Holiday Power Play

A Rivals to Lovers Hockey Romance Novella

Anne Martin

Content Warning

This book may contain content that is considered triggering to some. Please take care of yourself.

For a full list, go to: www.annemartinbooks.com

To the women who like their men to take charge.
Merry Christmas, you little ho ho ho.
Trevor's for you.

Chapter 1
Lana

Sometimes I wonder if men just get up in the morning, brush their teeth, look at their reflection in the mirror, and tell themselves, *"Today, I'm going to be a gigantic dick. And nobody's going to stop me."*

Or... maybe that's just my new neighbor.

The engine on his motorcycle revs as he pulls into the street.

I wonder when he'll notice that I'm, once again, occupying the parking spot that he's deemed to be his since moving into the empty townhome next door last week.

You see, I drive a small electric vehicle whose carbon footprint is nearly non-existent. I actually care about things like the environment and global warming and doing my part in leaving a healthy planet for future generations.

It doesn't make me a better person, by any means. But if it's a competition between who deserves the prime parking spot of the neighborhood—I think there's an obvious winner.

The prime spot sits between our two townhomes and just so happens to fit only two types of vehicles: a small electric car like mine. Or a motorcycle, like his. But I was here first, which means–I get to call dibs.

I peek out the corner of the blinds just above my bed and watch as he puts his bike into park across the street in a very inconvenient location. His movements are abrupt as he dismounts from the bike, tossing his leg over the side and yanking his gloves off his hands as he takes long strides up the sidewalk toward his house.

No wait... toward *my* house.

I try not to make any sudden movements that might alert him to my peeping Tom ways. I make sure the light stays off when I move the tiny sliver of the blind to try to catch him taking off his helmet before he enters his house at night. But he never does.

It's been nearly five days since the cocky guy moved in, replacing my sweet elderly neighbor whose family decided to move her into a nursing home due to a recent fall.

For her, I gladly parked across the street every day just so that she could have a more convenient parking spot to unload her groceries.

But this jerk–the one who revs his motorcycle at all hours of the night and blasts music that makes my walls vibrate and has a mouth that has no idea what an indoor voice sounds like when he's shouting at whatever game he and his dumb friends play–he deserves no such treatment.

I have no idea what the guy even looks like. I keep missing him when he leaves at random times during the day. And I've only been able to catch him coming back with a full-face helmet in place. Not that it makes any difference to me because I don't like him.

There's a loud knock at my door, and my heart nearly leaps into my throat.

Shit. It's him.

I melt off my bed and onto my floor, crawling on my hands and knees into the closet and hoping he'll just disappear. It's late. The sun is down. This would be a reasonable hour to assume that I'm in bed, not an hour to be knocking on your neighbor's door. *Rude.*

I bring my knees up to my chest and reach for the skates next to me. At least if he tries to break in, I can use the blade as a weapon.

There's another–more aggressive–knock. But I don't make any moves. Surely he knows I'm home given that my car is quite literally parked right up front. So he'll know I'm deliberately ignoring him.

But I could be in the shower. Or on a very important zoom meeting... or in the middle of the best sex of my life for all he knows, but instead he thinks he's entitled to knocking on my door at whatever hour he deems suitable.

Entitled brat.

The doorbell rings.

God, he's persistent. I suddenly regret not getting that doorbell camera on Black Friday like my brother insisted I should do. If I had it, I'd be able to just pick up my phone and tell him to go away because I'm busy.

But I'm not busy. I was just spying on him.

Another loud knock.

He's not going away. It's time to face this dick head-on. Besides, this isn't me. I don't shrink away from a fight. I might be living alone now, but that doesn't mean I'm not a grown ass woman that can handle her shit.

I stand and pull the robe off the hanger next to the unruly, fluffy white dress that's currently taking up most of the space in this closet. And as I make my way through the hall and down the stairs, I quickly palm my hair into submission before flipping on the porch light and opening the door with vigor.

"What do you want?" I hiss out, making sure not to hold back my disdain to him pounding on my door so late.

My new neighbor stands there, helmet tucked under an arm, his leather jacket hooked at the end of his fingers and strewn across one shoulder– bright amber-colored eyes look up at me.

His hair is a light brown that looks like he's spent a lot of time in the sun, and of course he's handsome as all get out. A squared jaw like that is hard to come by. It's just my luck that a guy I can't stand would move in next door and he also looks like... *wait, why does he look so familiar?*

"Hi," he says with a smile. The man has dimples. Again, just my luck.

"Is there a reason you're banging on my door?" I say, skipping the pleasantries.

"Yes," he says. "There's been some kind of misunderstanding with the parking, it seems." He motions toward my car.

"There sure is," I say, crossing my arms in front of my chest, leaning against my doorframe.

"It's mine," we both say to each other.

I push off the doorframe. "Look, Mr..."

"Sincaid," he says, almost reluctantly. "Trevor Sincaid."

Trevor Sinc—oh my freakin' god! Of course he looks familiar. He's all this city has been talking about for days. I've seen the social media posts. And the fan-sightings. It's become quite the game around town to post a picture of the humiliated player anytime he's been spotted out in public.

"As in the rookie defenseman for the Houston Heatwave?" I ask, just to be sure.

4

He catches his bottom lip between his teeth in a look that says *"You caught me."*

"Well, Trevor Sincaid, I don't care how famous you are. You can't park in my parking spot."

"Mmm, see that's the thing, Ms...."

Now he waits for me to introduce myself.

"MacDonald," I say, just as reluctantly.

He pauses, quickly assessing me from head to toe and narrows his eyes.

"Any relation to Vance MacDonald?" he asks.

"You mean my brother who plays on your team. Yeah... some relation."

"No shit! You're Mick's sister?" His eyes rove me up and down again, and I pull my robe tighter across my body.

When I just stare back at him blankly, he continues, "Well, you see Ms. MacDonald, the realtor who sold me the place said that I got the reserved parking in front of my house."

"Well, that's funny because there is no reserved parking in front of your house. It's in front of our houses which means it doesn't belong to any one of them. It's been first come, first serve ever since I moved in."

He just stands there, shifting from one foot to the other. "That's great and all, except... it's mine. It came with the house."

"I don't know what to tell you, Mr. Sincaid. Your realtor lied to you."

"Mm, I'm pretty sure I wouldn't have bought the place if it didn't come with it's own parking."

"Well," I say, leaning in further. "That sounds like a problem that you should take up with your realtor."

"Move your car," he says sternly.

"No," I scoff. "You just got here. You can't go around

throwing your name around like it holds any weight around here."

He takes in a deep breath. "Move your car or I'll call the city to remove it for you."

I step out onto my porch. "Are you threatening to have it towed?"

"If that's what it'll take to get you to move it from my parking."

"It isn't your parking," I almost scream out in frustration. But I keep my cool. Because this entitled, ridiculously handsome but very stupid boy will *not* win.

He shakes his head. "I was hoping we could do this the nice way." He reaches into his pocket and fishes out his phone. He looks up at me through dark lashes, "Last chance, neighbor."

"I dare you to call them," I grit out.

"Suit yourself." He dials a number and brings the phone up to his ear as he turns around and gives me his back. It's a nice back–strong and coiled muscles stretch out the shirt he's currently wearing.

The guy obviously works out. Not that I haven't noticed before. I've watched Trevor play. He's really good. Especially at checking the other players into the boards and landing him a seat in the penalty box. His team loves his tenacity–I should know–my brother won't stop talking about him, along with the rest of Houston.

But what I can't stand is how cocky and entitled he is. Especially after the little stunt he pulled recently. A little stunt that I personally know the consequences for.

"I wouldn't do that if I were you."

He turns to look at me from over his shoulder, but doesn't stop. "Hello, yes. I'd like to report a vehicle illegally parked in a reserved parking."

"You're going to regret that," I say, checking my nails as he continues.

"Uh yes, it's an ugly silver sardine can on wheels with the license plate number..." he pauses to read the plate, then looks at me, before spelling out "I-C-E-Q-W-N."

"It's Ice Queen," I say, remaining bored by his show of strength.

He shakes his head. "Yes, how long before you can get a truck out here?"

I roll my eyes. He probably didn't even call anyone.

"That's perfect. Thank you, John." He hangs up and turns back to me.

"Hope you like walking," he says with a wink, then steps onto the grassy patch between our two town homes and disappears into his house.

"What a knob," I say to myself, shutting the door to my house and locking it. He didn't call anyone.

I go back to my room where I pull out my phone to shoot a text to my brother. But he's already beat me to it.

> VANCE
>
> You all packed up for a Hallmark Christmas in the mountains?

> ME
>
> Depends... were you ever going to tell me that your teammate moved in next door?

> VANCE:
>
> ???

7

> ME
>
> Don't play dumb. I know you know.

> VANCE
>
> I don't keep track of all my teammates and their dwellings, Lana.

> ME
>
> You would if they were your favorite teammate. He's a total dick, by the way. He just pretended to call a towing service to get me to move my car.

> VANCE
>
> Did it work?

> ME
>
> No. I'm not an idiot. That's my parking spot.

> VANCE
>
> Of course it is.

You know what I don't like his tone. I dial him.

"What?" Vance says in a huff.

"What do you mean *of course it is?*"

"Look, I know you better than most people and you gotta admit, you can be a little..."

"Confident? Self-assured?"

"Confrontational," he says.

I blow raspberries. "I can't help it if I'm right about most things."

"So you're fighting with Sincaid?" he asks like he's just been severely inconvenienced.

"He started it. He just moved in and he's already walking around like he calls the shots," I spit out.

"Sounds about right. Well, that's just great."

"Yeah, why's that?"

I hear the sound of a truck beeping outside. There's no way. I peek out the window and shit... it looks like I was wrong. He *did* call a tow truck.

Vance continues, "It's just, he's having kind of a rough time and I told him he could–"

"That dick!" I interrupt him.

"You okay?"

I scramble to slip on some shoes as I make my way down the stairs and to the front door. "Your precious teammate called a fucking towing company on me!"

"He actually did it?"

"Hey!" I call out to the guy already loading my car.

"Lana, calm down." Vance says, "I'm sure it's just a misunder–"

"I gotta go." I hang up the call and wave my arms frantically at the truck driver. "Hey!"

I run up to him. "That's my car! And this is my spot!" I tell him.

The guy is wearing a jumpsuit and looks me up and down and rolls his neck before answering me. "Look lady. I just do what I'm told. You have a problem. Take it up with the city."

He reaches into his pocket and pulls out a notepad, ripping the first page on it and hands it to me.

"Are you fucking kidding me?"

He shrugs and moves to the cabin of his truck.

"You can't take my car. I *need* my car." I reach for the door handle and try to tug at it to try to open it. I remember reading somewhere that it's illegal to tow a car if there's somebody in it.

But it's locked. I wonder if the same rules apply if I'm sitting *on* it.

Anne Martin

I jump onto the hood and sit on it, my legs crisscrossed like I'm about to practice some yoga.

The driver looks at me. "Ma'am, the car's already loaded. You want me to unload it? There's a fee."

"Are you crazy? I'm not paying you to unload it. I didn't ask for it to be loaded in the first place!"

I watch the door to my neighbor's house swing open. He's no longer in jeans, boots and a leather jacket. Now he's in cozy grey sweats and–*fuck me*–completely shirt-less. The deep cut of the v of his abs is visible for all to see.

"Hey," he waves to the tow truck operator. "You must be John. Is there a problem here?" His eyes flick over to me.

"Is there a problem here?" I mimic him. "Of course there's a fucking problem here–you!"

John looks up at him and then does a double take when he sees who it is.

"Oh wow!" he laughs to himself. "I know you! You're Trevor Sincaid!" The man's bored face morphs into an excited expression much akin to a child on Christmas morning.

He can't be serious right now? Does everyone love this jackass?

Trevor walks up to the front of my car and stuffs his hands into his pocket. "Yep, that's me."

"Unload my car at once!" I say to the driver, ignoring the obnoxious player, and waving a menacing finger.

Trevor looks at me with an amused smirk. "Don't think that's going to do much. Money talks, Ms. MacDonald." Then he turns to the tow truck operator. "Isn't that right, John?"

John, much to his surprise, seems to be elated that the professional hockey player remembered his name. "Tell you what, I'll waive the fee if you're willing to give me an autograph. My son's a big fan."

Trevor's lips purse in consideration. "Hmm... I don't know. How would my illegally parked neighbor learn her lesson?"

"Learn my lesson?" I yell at him from the hood of my car. "I lived here long before you ever did, you epic dickhead."

Both men look at each other and shrug.

God, I can't stand the male species. They do these ridiculous things to piss us off and then wonder why we're so mad at them like we're the crazy ones. *They* make us crazy. By doing shit like this.

"Maybe if she promises to keep her can of sardines out of my parking spot... I'll consider rescuing her," Trevor decides.

He has this look in his eye. A dare. One that says, *what are you going to do now?*

"I don't need to be rescued. Especially not by a ridiculous, self-entitled, nepo baby." I stay seated on my hood.

John shrugs. "Well then, I'm going to need you to get off the vehicle ma'am. I'd really like to just get home to my wife and kids if you don't mind."

"Oh, don't do that, John. Don't make it seem like I'm the bad guy here. It was your hockey hero that called you out here in the first place. If you want to put the blame on anyone–blame him."

Trevor cocks his head at me. "I wouldn't have had to call John, and keep him from his sweet family, if you would've just moved your car like I asked. Very nicely, might I add."

"You call pounding on my door at eight 'o clock at night asking nicely? You need your head checked."

"Ma'am, if you don't get off the hood of this vehicle–"

11

"*My* vehicle," I stress. "It's *my* vehicle, so I'll sit on the hood whenever I damn well please. And I'll park here whenever I please, because it's my parking spot. So no. I'm not moving."

John gives Trevor a look. They're communicating telepathically and I don't appreciate it.

"You know what," I say, making a decision. I jump off the car and land right between the two of them. "You want my car so bad, John. Just take it."

I push past the defenseman and strut over to the front door of my house. I don't need to turn around to know that Trevor's looking at me, watching my every move.

And I hope he gets a good look, because he has no idea what's coming for him.

Chapter 2
Trevor

"There he is! The man of the hour," my team captain, Keelan Landry, sets down his mat and stretches it out. "Glad you could join us."

"Yeah, well. I ran into a little... inconvenience," I say, taking an empty spot on the gym floor.

"Uh oh. Sounds like The Rookie may have met someone," Michael Ferguson, one of our forwards comments from the other side of the gym.

The whole team is here tonight. We've been getting a lot of injuries lately and coach has arranged for a mandatory stretch session three times a week to keep us agile. With our crazy schedule this week and Christmas just two days away, he called this last minute session.

"Oh, he met someone alright," Vance MacDonald sets his mat next to me. "And she told me all about it."

"To be fair, I didn't know she was your sister," I tell him. "At first."

"A sister? Oh shit... here we go again," Zane O'Connor, fellow defenseman says.

Our starting goalie walks behind me, slapping my back

13

with a heavy hand. "Haven't you learned your lesson with sisters, Rookie?" Ryker says, voice low.

"Yes, I absolutely have. Which is why I have no interest in her in that way." I turn to MacDonald, or Mick, as we like to call him. "Seriously, you don't have to worry about that."

Mick laughs. "Dude, you don't know my sister. She's not the kind of girl you want to mess with. And if you ask me, calling a tow truck on her–automatically puts you on her naughty list. She hates you."

"Well, I'm not a fan either," I mutter.

Mick shakes his head. "That's too bad."

"Because she's my neighbor?"

His eyes twinkle. "Amongst other things."

"Other things? What other things?" I say, watching him.

Coach Murray bursts through the doors. "Alright boys, let's get this done so we can get on with our Christmas plans."

"What other things?" I whisper to Mick whose suddenly decided to drop the conversation.

He presses a finger to his lips and points to Coach Murray up front.

An hour of stretches later, we're splayed out on our mats, dripping in sweat when Mick rolls over to look at me.

"So about the trip tomorrow..."

Oh yes. The trip. The one he invited me to join him on since last week's calendar debacle in NYC.

We had these calendars we were trying to sell at a book-store event when Mick had the genius idea for us to take our shirts off. We all agreed it would make sense–it was a hockey romance event after all.

But I was the one who took it a step too far. One of our

patrons and loyal fans asked me to take a picture with her in only my underwear.

Who am I to turn down a fan? I was already a half-dressed Christmas elf, what was one more article of clothing?

I'll tell you what... it was what got us kicked out of the event, plastered all over social media and now I can't go anywhere without someone mentioning the Heatwave rookie with Santa's package delivery living in his underwear.

Was it inappropriate to strip down in a public place? Yes. But did I do it for the fans? Also yes. So why am I the one being punished and asked to lie low during Christmas this year?

Those were the words from our team's PR manager, Rina Lopez. *"Just lie low this Christmas. Maybe leave town. Your stupidity will be forgotten."*

Hence why Mick invited me to the mountains for Christmas with his family. We leave tomorrow.

"Wait..." I flop to my side to look at him. "Your sister is coming, isn't she?"

"She wasn't going to... but she called me earlier and told me that her car got impounded. So... yeah. It looks like she's joining us."

I groan. "Well, does she know I'm coming?"

"She will," he says, pushing himself up and stretching a hand out to me.

"Gah... I wish I would've known that before I had her car towed."

"You just had to be a dick to Lana," Mick says, hauling me up.

Huh. So her name's Lana. Pretty.

"I mean, she's not very nice herself."

Even if she's quite literally the most beautiful woman I've ever laid eyes on. Her ridiculous personality kind of ruins the whole vibe for me.

When I saw Lana MacDonald–*why does that sound like a clown name?* Well, when she pulled the door open to her town home I almost changed my mind and was willing to drop the whole parking spot situation.

In the grand scheme of things. It wasn't that big a deal. But then she opened her mouth and I thought better about it.

She'd run me over with her tiny car the first chance she got if I showed her even an ounce of weakness.

"Give her a chance, man. Lana's had a rough month. And you calling a tow truck on her... that was the disgusting maraschino cherry on top."

"What? I love maraschino cherries," I tell him, grabbing the backpack I dropped off at the entrance next to my helmet and swinging it onto my back.

"Yeah, well Lana doesn't. She hates cherries."

I'll file that valuable information away for later. Just in case.

"I could just fly to Breckenridge... I don't want to be the third wheel."

"Technically, Lana is the third wheel. She wasn't planning on coming out this year. But like I said, she's had a rough month."

"Is that supposed to make me feel like a total dick for fighting her on the parking spot thing. Because it's not working," I inform him.

I push the door open to the exit of the gym and hold it out for him.

"Yes, you should. But don't worry, she'll make sure you don't get away with it," he gives me a reassuring wink.

"Awesome," I mutter.

We're walking out of the gym and to our parking spots. The cool Texas air blows through my wet head reminding me that it really is winter. Even if it hasn't felt cold enough here to embrace it lately. His crossover SUV is parked right next to my motorcycle.

"I don't know man... maybe we can just forget the whole thing. Rina asked me to lie low. I can just stay home."

"And eat ramen noodles on Christmas day because you don't cook? I won't let you do that."

Mick is a big guy. One of those guys that you're scared of going head to head with on ice. But off the ice, he's just a giant Canadian teddy bear I call my friend. His bright green eyes against his mocha skin stay glued on me, waiting for a response.

"It's a family event. And I'm not family. I don't want to crash a family event."

"It's not crashing when you're literally getting invited," Mick says. "You just don't want to deal with Lana. Understandably so, I know she can be a lot. But you'll regret it if you don't come. Almost everyone is leaving town. Who will you spend Christmas with?"

My own family doesn't really do Christmas, they're all over the US and all too busy with their own lives to ever come together. It'd be nice to just be apart of a family that does.

Christmas with my friend's family doesn't sound so bad. I'd be lying low in the mountains and away from the city where I can't go anywhere without being spotted. Doing exactly what my superiors want. And if the cabin is as big as Mick has alluded to, I'll barely have to interact with Lana anyways.

"Fine," I relent. "How long is this road trip anyway?"

"One day if we just drive straight through, which is what I plan to do."

I swipe a hand down my face. One day. Two if we consider the drive back. Two full days on the road with my teammate, for a Christmas where I'm not alone with my sad little tree that's sitting on my kitchen table, eating ramen, and watching Elf on repeat.

I imagine a home-cooked meal, warm fireplaces, and laughter. Lots of laughter.

And I want it. Damn near need it.

"Ok. Let's take this road trip, I guess," I say, turning to my bike and slipping onto it.

"Great! I'll be by your place at four to pick you up."

I'm hiking a leg over my bike when he says that so I must've misheard him. I stay staring at him, holding my helmet as he tosses his bag into his car.

"What?" he asks, arm resting on the hood of his car.

"Four... in the afternoon, right?"

Mick's brows furrow. Even in the dark, I can see his eyes questioning me.

"Right?" I say again.

"No, man. You don't drive straight through from Houston to Breckenridge by leaving at four in the afternoon. If I were you, I'd get home and get packing if you haven't already." He slips into the seat of his car and starts backing out before I get a chance to ask him more questions.

How long will we be gone? What should I pack for? How are we dividing up the drive?

But Mick is gone before I can say a word. It's fine. I'm sure we can figure it out in the morning. My biggest question though is what will Lana do when she finds out?

* * *

What feels like just a few hours later, there's a car honking obnoxiously outside on the street.

Who the hell is honking at... I look at my phone and I see the time. 4:06.

The horn honks again.

I toss the sheets aside and quickly type out a text telling him to shut the hell up and I'm coming.

It takes me less than five minutes to be out the door and my teammate greets me with the biggest smile on his face. "Morning, sunshine!"

Jeez. Did he even sleep?

I yawn. "You can call me that in three hours when the sun is actually up."

"I got you a coffee," he says, motioning to the steaming cup sitting between us in the cupholder.

"That was nice of you," I say, grabbing it and taking that delicious first sip. It feels like Christmas. Warm and cozy and—my god—is that peppermint?

"Listen, if you plan to have me switch off at some point, I'm going to need much more than a peppermint mocha. I need sleep."

He grabs his phone and dials someone.

For a moment, I forget it's not just us.

Ms. Grinch-i-pants will be joining the mountain crew party too. And since we didn't exactly leave off on the best terms last night–considering the whole her car being impounded situation–I don't anticipate she'll be in a good mood when she sees me.

But what do I know? It's Christmas, and there is such a thing as miracles. At least for my sake I'd like to hope that there is. Plus, I guess I can be the bigger person and apologize.

I'll consider it.

"Hey," Mick's voice fills the car. "Yeah that's me. You were supposed to be up. Please tell me you packed."

I watch a light come on in the upstairs window of her townhome. A room that seems to share a wall with my own. I wonder if she can hear me at all. I don't recall ever hearing her.

Mick tells her to hurry up or he's leaving her and hangs up.

"What'd the little grinch say when you told her I was coming?" I yawn out.

"Uh... she... well she..." Mick pops the trunk open and opens the door to leave.

"Mick?" I call out to him as he shuts the door. "You told her right?" I call out louder so he can hear me.

He smirks and walks off.

Great. She doesn't know. She's going to take one look at me and banish me from the car.

The light turns off in the room upstairs and another comes on that lights up the window on the front door.

She doesn't have any Christmas lights or wreathes decorating her house. To be fair, I don't either.

But on her side there are dead plants that need to be replaced and an overgrown bush that is creeping its way to the front door, making her place not only not welcoming but a little creepy.

It's very on brand for what I've already come to know about my friend's moody sister.

The front door opens and she rolls her luggage down the pathway, absentmindedly looking down at her phone. Her thick brown curls crown her face in a halo.

That face.

Her skin is much lighter than her brother's and she has a splash of freckles across her nose. And unlike her brother's green eyes, she has chocolate eyes with an exotic almond shape that makes her overall look just–captivating.

But I'm not seeing all these details right now. I just know from the initial sight of her last night that is what I can expect.

She rolls her suitcase all the way down the sidewalk, dragging a big garment bag along with her.

Deep breath. Here we go.

Chapter 3
Lana

The air is much cooler this morning than it has been all month. Christmas is in the air.

Awesome.

I'm not normally this moody. But after my jackass of a neighbor pulled his little car stunt last night–it didn't exactly put me in the Christmas spirit.

It does however, put me in the spirit to break a bunch of shit. If only I didn't have to sell or pawn everything off just to keep afloat this month.

Which is why as I'm taking a step at a time with my luggage with one arm, I'm also hauling the giant waste of space that's been sitting in my closet in the other arm.

I don't exactly know why I waited this long to get rid of the dress. I spent plenty of wine drunk nights crying, watching cringey rom-coms and occasionally looking at it hanging there from my closet door—a stinging reminder that I wouldn't be the girl that gets the happy ending.

Not for now. And honestly, maybe not ever.

Vance rounds his SUV all smiles. He was always the early bird between the two of us.

"Can I help you, Lani Banani?" He reaches for the heavy pile of white fabric hiding under a black garment bag.

I let him take it. "There are two boxes by the door if you wanna grab those, too."

"Sheesh, you weren't kidding when you said you needed to bring a few things."

"Yeah, well mom said she has a friend whose daughter is having a shotgun wedding and will be so pleased to get a wedding in a box. Her words."

He pops the trunk open and the first thing I see is twice the luggage I expected for my brother.

"I thought you said it was just a four day trip—why are you packing like you're gone until New Years?"

The sound of a voice clearing draws my attention to the front seat, occupied by the last person I'd expect to see sitting there, considering my *very* vocal rebukes of the player. Rebukes that I have not withheld from my brother.

"Hi," Trevor Sincaid says with a crooked smile and gentle wave.

I slam the trunk shut and turn abruptly to my brother.

"Why the hell is *he* here?"

Vance just looks at me. His eyes trying to tell me all the things his mouth won't say.

Don't be like this, Lana.

He was lonely, Lana.

Be nice, Lana.

"Absolutely not," I say to his wordless expressions.

"Look..." he starts.

"Absolutely *not!*" I grab my luggage and start rolling it back to my front door.

"And just how do you plan on getting to Breck then?"

I turn to look at him. "Oh, I'm a smart woman, V. I'm

sure I can figure it out. But this..." I point to the guy in the front seat. "It's not happening."

The passenger door opens and Trevor steps out of the waiting vehicle. "I-is there a problem here?"

"No," Vance says, at the same time I say, "Hell yes, there's a problem!"

"Let me guess," Trevor says, leaning against the car and sliding his hands into his pocket. "Mick didn't tell you about me coming, did he?" He shoots my brother a glare.

Vance pops open the trunk again. "Fine, you caught me. I knew that if I told either one of you, you wouldn't want to come, okay? But look, we're all up and it's a beautiful day."

"How would you know? Sun's not even up yet," I murmur.

"That's what I said," Trevor adds.

"And we are all grown-ups," my brother continues. "Who can share a small space temporarily for the sake of having a great Christmas, right?"

Trevor and I stare at each other as I stand near the front door of my townhome, ready to just call it. I'm not doing this. His eyes are a soft brown, and even wearing a hoodie, I can see the sun-bleached brown of his hair poking out like he just ran a hand through it after waking up.

"I, for one, have no problem with any of that," Trevor says, grinning. His cheeks reveal two dimples that do nothing but further irritate me.

"Well, I would rather collect loose change from the streets to pay for a flight."

Which is exactly what I plan to do.

"La-na," Vance drags out my name. "Come on. By midnight, we'll be in a giant cabin in the mountains and you won't have to see him if you don't want to."

Trevor looks over at Vance confused, then back at me. "Why do I have the feeling you have something against me?"

I groan as I drag my luggage back toward my waiting brother at the back of his car.

"Because I do. I have a lot of somethings against you, Trevor Sincaid."

Vance drops the handles down and tosses my luggage into the trunk, rearranging things to make space for the other boxes.

"Glad we can be civil," he says to me, before heading back up the steps to retrieve the rest of my failed wedding belongings.

Trevor comes up to me.

"Are you going to tell me what those somethings are?" he asks like a curious puppy. A very cute, curious puppy. *Damn him.*

"Do you have a week?" I say, all bite.

"No, but I have four days and a really great attention span."

"Great, because I'll need every minute of those four days if you want to know all the reasons why I find you to be obnoxious, entitled, and everything that's wrong in professional sports."

I turn on my heel and open the back door, tossing my purse in.

"Okay," he says thoughtfully. "Listen, I can take the back seat, if you want to sit next to your brother," he says, appearing at my side again.

I can already see he has a very keen, inability to take a hint.

"I'd rather not have to interact with either of you at the moment. Thanks."

25

He backs up with hands surrendered, just as Vance tosses the last of my belongings into the trunk.

He shuts it and slides into the drivers seat. Trevor takes his spot in the passenger seat and Vance looks back at me, excitedly. "Ready?"

I don't grace him with a smile, instead I just stare at him with a blank expression on my face.

"I am!" my older brother says, ignoring me. He turns his attention to the radio and puts it on a Holiday station. As he pulls out from the parking in front of my town home, his teammate looks back at me.

His hoodie is still up and it's dark except for the small glow of the dashboard. I refuse to look directly at him, as I cross my arms over my chest and stare out the window.

But my body is fully aware of the way he's studying me. From my peripheral I can see his eyes taking me in. They study my black curls, drag down the length of my athleisurewear, down my legs then back up, before he quirks up a smile and turns his body to face the windshield.

It's fast, the way his eyes soaked me up. But somehow it felt like time slowed as he watched me.

And I want him to know I don't approve.

"You got a problem with the way I look?" I say to him.

Vance glances at me through the rearview mirror, brows cinched together.

"You know, if I wanted to die by way of looks I could've just gone to work today," Trevor says, not turning to face me.

"We can still make that happen. Space City Arena is just down the road. Care to make a pit stop brother and dump some unwanted baggage?"

"Ouch," Trevor says, holding his chest in mock offense. "You know, I'm starting to think maybe I'm not welcome."

"Starting?" I scoff. "Took you long enough."

Vance reaches for the volume knob and turns it down.

"Nope. We're not doing this. It's Christmas, people. We need to be nice or at least pretend to be or we can just forget about the whole trip."

"I'm not doing anything," Trevor says, cocking his head my way.

I glare at him, doing my best to keep my clenched fists out of his view.

I know his type. Athletic. Charming. They win everyone with their dimples and abs. It doesn't matter if they're just walking dicks in the shape of men.

When I don't say anything else, Vance puts the music back up. I dig my phone out of my backpack. Mom's already shot over her "safe travels" text to Vance and I in a group chat.

I pull up her contact and type out a message just to her.

ME

Did you know about the Sincaid situation?

Mom's text comes in right away.

MOM

He's hot, right? *winky face*

Oh my god. My mother knew. She knew and didn't tell me. Despite everything I've tried to communicate to her about the Trevor Sincaid's of the world and my complete and total disdain for them.

It's easy to just accept his type when your entire career isn't built on fighting him and the inequalities in the sports world.

I take a deep breath as I try to calmly type out my next words.

ME

> Mom. No. We can't just let him crash our Christmas. This is insane. Why didn't anybody tell me?

MOM

> Lana, your brother called and said he had a friend in need. We aren't just going to leave him out on the streets.

ME

> In need?! The guy makes bank, mom. Even as a new player. He wasn't going to be "out on the streets."

Please. I'm supposed to feel sorry for the lonely hockey star whose bare body graces the pages of a well known calendar and whose entitlement got my car impounded? I feel no sympathy.

MOM

> You know what I mean, Lana. Since when have we ever been a family that turns people away?

> If we were, you and Vance wouldn't be here.

I roll my eyes.

Vance and I are adopted. It's very clear that we are just by looking at a family photo. My dad is built like a viking and has long-hippy like hair that he wears in a man-bun. He wears flannels year-round and has a laugh that can rattle windows.

My mom has a delicate look to her with porcelain, doll-like skin and bright blue eyes and golden hair. And though she looks petite, especially when she's standing next to my brother and father—the woman is a force.

Vance has dark skin, brown curly hair and bright green eyes.

And me? I have mocha eyes, caramel skin and freckles. Lots of freckles. I never knew my real parents. Vance knew his, but refused to ever talk about them. We were just six and five when the MacDonald's took us in.

But where Vance and I grew up, we were always given assessing looks by complete strangers as we walked hand in hand with our parents. We didn't fit the description of what they would expect a typical Canadian family to look like.

And I may or may not have developed a really defensive way of approaching the world because of it. I don't take kindly to people assessing me. And so far, not even twenty minutes into this trip, that's all my brother's "downtrodden" friend seems to be doing.

Assessing me.

I choose not to further engage with my mom at the moment. She always looks at the glass half full and I have a problem with that. Because of course she would. People take one good look at Janie MacDonald and they want to help her. They want to make life easy for her. Mom doesn't know a world where people see her as a threat just by merely existing.

I feel the prickle of awareness on the back of my neck that tells me I'm being watched and I look up from my phone to see those light brown eyes on me again. The color in them is soft like amber.

At the sight of him I drop my phone and he reaches down at the same time that I do.

"Can you not invade the air I breathe?" I say to him.

He looks at me, smirking as he hands me the phone. "Jeez. I was just trying to help. You texting Santa to make sure he adds me to the naughty list?"

"Oh, trust me. You're already at the top of that list."

"Good to know I make such an impression."

I can already tell this trip is going to be hell.

"You make an impression the same way a small rock inside my shoe would," I say back.

"Impossible to ignore?" he offers, with a small pull in the corner of his lips.

"Annoying," I say, turning away from him again.

Somehow that seems to please him, because from my peripheral I can see him still staring at me with that stupidly handsome grin.

"What?" I bark out.

"I'm ready to hear all the reasons why I'm the actual worst whenever you're ready," he says.

Vance gives him a glance. "Are you a masochist? Just leave well enough alone man," he says.

"No, your sister decided after one look at me that I'm the human equivalent of a vending machine that takes your money and never gives you what you pay for so I want to know why."

I internally applaud him for his creativity in the realm of analogies. That's exactly how I see him.

Vance just shakes his head. "Your funeral."

Trevor turns his attention back to me. "So? Let me have it."

I glare at him. "Well, should we start with the fact that you rose to the top because your daddy has more money than he knows what to do with so securing deals for his precious kids to get everything they want has become his own personal sport?"

He tilts his head but waits for me to say more.

"Or should we start with the fact that the only reason you're with the Heatwave is because you used your ex to help you get a spot on the team and then left her once you got what you wanted?"

He opens his mouth like he's about to say something then shuts it immediately, motioning for me to go on.

"Or," I say, "should we talk about how athletes like you are the very reason that I wake up everyday to teach a sport to young girls who all they want is to be taken seriously when their male counterparts just take their shirts off and get deals without ever having to prove their worth?"

"Is that what you think?" Trevor finally speaks up. "That I didn't get here on my own merits?"

"You're everything that's wrong in professional sports—flashy male athletes that dominate headlines while women who are far more talented constantly get overlooked. Never to be taken seriously. If we were to do half the things guys like you do, we'd be dropped from the sport without a second thought."

His body is now fully twisted toward me, "Careful little grinch, if I didn't know any better I'd say you were jealous."

"Jealous?!" I scoff. "Please I'm stating facts, Sincaid. If you're too dense to realize it, then that sounds like a personal problem. And the name's Lana MacDonald."

"Hm, sounds like a clown's name," he retorts.

"The only clown in this car is you," I bark back.

"Okay, you two..." Vance chimes in.

"No," Trevor says, putting his hand up. "She wants to pretend she knows everything about me, then let's do this. And allow me to set the record straight."

Chapter 4
Trevor

W hat Lana MacDonald—*I still can't get over that name*—doesn't know is that she's only half right.

No, I did not just get by because my dad is rich, though I can't say the same about my brothers and their careers.

And if she really thinks I used Izzy because of her connection to the Heatwave—then she's more delusional than I can ever help her see.

But she's not wrong about women having a harder time in sports. You don't have to look too far to know that is a stone cold truth. One that my own mother had to face as a woman's hockey player.

And if Lana MacDonald did more than just run that pretty little mouth of hers, then maybe she would see that the reason I'm even playing hockey today is *because* of a woman—one that's so much like her, it's a little scary.

"So tell me then, Lana, what makes me entitled versus someone like your brother?"

"God, please no. Don't bring me into this," Mick says, lifting a hand from the steering wheel and shaking it at me.

"What? It's a solid argument. Why am I the problem and not just every male athlete ever? We were both selected from college. We both play for the same team. How am I the problem and not Mick here?"

"I didn't say you were the problem," Lana protests.

"No, you did. Just in so many more words."

Mick knocks the back of his head against the head rest a few times and shoots me a glare.

"You know what. The very fact that I have to explain this to you, is why you are the problem," she says with finality. She's sitting arms crossed and not looking at me as she does.

"So that's it? You're done talking to me."

Her eyes glide to mine only momentarily. But she quickly looks away again.

Clearly we're done here. Lana has officially shut down.

I sigh deep and heavy before turning away from her and looking out my window.

A few hours go by with Mick just jumping from music station to music station. And the sun has slowly risen up over the horizon to my right just as I'm trying to get comfortable and fall asleep.

I flip to the other side and catch a glimpse of Lana. She's also asleep. Her body folded across the back seat and she's using her baby blue sweatshirt as a pillow. Her dark curls are spirally and wild and have fallen over her face, a few strands sticking to her glossed lips. Pink, full lips. Pink, snarky, stupidly tempting... lips.

Mick clears his throat, and I realize that he's caught me staring at his sister.

"What?" I murmur.

"I didn't say anything." He grins and messes with the stations again.

He skips over a song I like and I sit up straighter. "Oh, put it back, put it back."

Mick gives me a look. "Seriously?"

"Yes, seriously! Change it back, Mick."

The radio plays *Stargazing* by Myles Smith and I sing aloud to the chorus.

The grinch laying in the backseat stirs and slowly rises, just as Mick joins me in singing too.

The song ends and I look back to see her face buried into the sweatshirt she was just using as a pillow. Her shoulders have the gentlest shake to them, and for a second, it looks like she might be crying. She takes a deep breath before pulling the sweatshirt away from her face revealing wet, red eyes.

She *was* crying. She quickly wipes her face and breathes in deeply before meeting my eyes.

"Man, I really gotta pee," Mick says, breaking up our shared gaze. He hasn't picked up on his sister's tears. "I'm just going to pull over here."

He pulls the car into a tiny gas station off the highway in a small town that I'd never considered stopping in.

"I'm good," I say, pulling the hoodie down off my head. "Lana?"

She clears her throat. "Nothing for me. Thanks, V."

"Alright, well. Text me if you guys change your minds. And try not to kill each other," he adds, shutting the door behind him as he bounds to the entrance of the gas station.

I turn to Lana. "Was it the song?"

She takes another deep breath. "I'm fine."

I don't believe her for a second. "That's literally what every woman says when they're *not* fine."

"I'm not every woman, Sincaid."

I watch as she looks out the window avoiding me again.

"Stargazing is a pretty romantic song... maybe it made you think of an old fling?"

"Stop digging. You're not going to find out so just stop."

"Alright, little grinch. You've been burned that much is clear."

"And none of your business," she adds.

"And none of my business," I agree.

"So let's not keep doing this," she says, motioning between us.

"Talking?" I harrumph. "My bad, let me stop being a friendly human to the grumpy woman who happens to be related to one of my best friends. It's called being nice, Lana."

"I don't want your niceties, Trevor. I want your silence."

"Well that's too bad," I say, pushing the door open to the SUV. I slam it shut and round the vehicle, popping back up at the driver's seat. "Because now I'm driving and it's driver's choice."

"Driver's choice?" She parrots questioningly, arms crossing over her chest.

"Yes, and in order to stay awake, we're going to play a game to get to know each other." I pull the mirror down a bit and glare at her through it.

"I'm out of here," she says, pushing her door open and sliding out. Without saying another word, she slams the door and stomps over to the mini-mart entrance, swinging the door open as she glares back at me and disappears.

"Tough crowd," I mutter to myself.

I didn't ask for this. And right about now I feel an anger boiling in my stomach at the way this girl is treating me. I mean, what the hell did I personally do to her to become the villain here? The whole parking debacle aside, she decided I was the bad guy before she even met me.

I get it if she doesn't like me because I'm a male athlete in professional sports. One who she assumes had it easy because she doesn't have the whole story. But Lana doesn't know the half of it.

She doesn't know that mom already had me practicing in little mites at four years old, falling on my ass over and over and over until I was too sore to sit. Or that by the time I was in middle school, I was hardly ever home. I was traveling and hoping to get scouted. My mom was the one driving me everywhere, making sure that I was always the best. That I was the one the scouts watched.

My mom was—until very recently—my agent.

And I trusted her more than anyone to help me get to the top. The only problem is that I wanted her as my mom even more.

Life in sports is tough. People are constantly criticizing you. People always have opinions. Case in point: the beautiful ice queen I'm now stuck sharing a small vehicle with.

There's a knock on the window. Mick is back.

"*Sup?*" I mouth to him.

"You driving?" he says, muffled by the glass between us. I nod at him, and he pumps his fist.

I expect him to occupy the seat next to me, but instead, he opens the door to the back seat and slides in. The top of his head almost hits the roof of the car.

"That's great because I need a nap."

He hands me a paper cup.

"Why do you keep buying me drinks?" I ask, eyeing it in his hand.

"It's hot chocolate. I'm trying to set the tone."

I take it from him. "For what exactly?"

"For the rest of this trip, man. I need you and Lana to be

sweet, warm, and in the Christmas spirit. Because up until now, I regret bringing either of you."

I take a sip of the proffered cup. And I can't help the way my face scrunches at the taste.

"Blech... well, you'll have to do better than gas station hot chocolate. Jeez, what's in this shit? Diesel?"

Mick laughs as he opens a bag of pretzels and pops a few into his mouth. "I knew you'd hate it."

I give him a look through the mirror, and I watch as he turns his face, and it drops. "Quick, lock the doors."

"What? Why?"

"Now!"

I do as he says, just as his sister approaches the back door and pulls on the handle. Mick shakes his head at her and points to the passenger seat. She slams a fist against his window, and he barks out a laugh again.

"For somebody that wants us to get along, you're really setting us up for success here," I deadpan.

Lana rounds the back of the car and appears at the window across from me. I kindly unlock the door, and the second she pulls it open, I blurt out, "It was your brother!"

She slides in and slams the door shut.

"I don't want to talk. I just want to get to Breckenridge and as far away from you as possible."

"Because I'm entirely irresistible, and you can't breathe around me?" I say, adding a playful smirk.

"Because if you say anything else, Sincaid. I might push you out of this moving vehicle."

"A homicidal Christmas. That's the spirit, Lana," Mick says from the back seat.

She glowers. "I'm sure we can come up with a great Christmas album along the lines of *Trevor got ran over by his teammate's sister*," I sing.

Nothing. I get no smile. No acknowledgment. Yeah, this officially really sucks. I'm sitting next to what just might be the world's most beautiful woman, and I can't even formulate coherent thoughts, let alone make her just fucking smile.

I settle on an instrumental station and pull away from the tiny roadside mini-mart.

An hour later, Mick is totally out snoring in the back seat, and I have to put the volume up higher just to drown him out.

Lana is scrolling through what looks like a photo album on her phone and deleting things as she does.

I notice they're pictures of her with a guy from my peripheral. Photos of the two of them together. Some of just him. One of him with Mick. She hesitates over that one. Like if she's not sure she should. But deletes it, too.

"So," I find myself saying into the dead silence, lowering the music.

The trees outside are rushing past us, and there's been a noticeable change in the terrain since leaving Houston. More greenery. Chiller air. The sun is up.

She shifts uncomfortably in her seat, legs crossing one over the other as she attempts to move further away from me.

"What?" she says when I don't continue.

"Was he a friend of Mick's?"

Her eyes flick to mine as she catches what I'm referring to.

"Do you make it a habit of yours to stick your nose where it doesn't belong?"

"Not just my nose," I tease.

"You're disgusting," she mutters.

"What? I was going to say my head, too," I say.

"Which head?"

I fake gasp. "Now, who's being disgusting?"

"Please," she mutters. "You players all talk the same. I've been around Vance and his friends my whole life. I know what you guys talk about the second a girl leaves your vicinity."

I sit up straighter, excited that she's actually engaging in conversation with me.

"Oh, do tell," I urge her.

She shakes her head. "You comment on her ass. Or her tits. Or where you'd like to dip your stick, and all of those remarks will never have anything to do with her as a woman. Her dreams. Her desires. And everything to do with you and yours."

A feminist... this should be fun.

"So what are your desires, Lana?"

"It was a hypothetical scenario," she explains.

"But this is a real question," I say back. "What are your desires?"

Did my voice just drop an octave? I didn't mean to do that. Something about the way the vixen is tugging at her bottom lip as she takes in my question has my body reacting in a way I can't even fully control.

She studies me a beat longer before answering. "In a perfect world?"

"Sure," I say. "In your perfect world."

"I'd want every little girl to get the same opportunities as every little boy. Regardless of their family's financial status. Or the color of their skin. I'd want them to achieve their dreams because they're good at what they do. Bottom line."

I was expecting to hear a different answer, but then again, this is the Ice Queen.

"And that's not something that's currently available?"

"No," she says sternly. "Not usually."

"Well, then, what needs to change?" I genuinely ask.

She adjusts in her seat again, this time, her body language opens up to me. I welcome the small gesture.

"It starts by not celebrating poor behavior," she says matter-of-factly, bringing her coffee cup to her lips and taking a sip. "By promoting athletes who earn their merits. And are true role models for the next generation. Not just turning a blind eye because someone happens to have a nice smile and washboard abs."

I look down at my midsection. "You think I have a nice smile and washboard abs?" I bait her.

She stops the coffee cup coming up to her mouth. "I think you're very attractive," she states, and I almost slam on the breaks at her admission. "Until you go and open your mouth," she adds, studying me before she takes another sip, her lips splitting in a pleased smile.

I roll my eyes and turn the volume back up but she reaches for the knob to change the station.

"What? Christmas music too cheerful for a Grinch?"

"Not really in the spirit," she says dryly.

"You don't say," I glance at her as she wriggles out of her sweatshirt. This time, the t-shirt underneath clings to it as she tries to slip it off, and I catch a glimpse of her midsection. She's so fit. Copper skin taut over muscles that show this woman knows hard work.

I'm so captivated by the sight that I don't see when the traffic comes to a complete stop ahead of us.

Lana frees herself from her sweatshirt prison, and the second her eyes take in the cars ahead, she yells, "Stop!"

I react just before I connect with the back of a black pickup truck. Mick riles from his slumber, muttering incomprehensible words as he shoots up from his resting position.

"Shit!" I breathe out as the entire vehicle jolts to a stop. I don't even realize when my arm instinctively shoots out to protect her from the impending hit, cupping a handful of her tender breast.

We all catch our breaths as the adrenaline hits. Our eyes meet briefly before Mick says, "You wanna take your hands off my sister's chest there, Sinc?"

She doesn't say anything; she just watches me as I snatch my hand away. "I'm so sorry," I rush out.

She puts a hand out, dismissing me as she takes in the scene around us. "What the hell is this?"

We hear distant honking at the sound of sirens down the road.

"Might be an accident." I open my car door and step out to get a good look. The truck in front of me doesn't have anybody in it, the driver seems to be approaching from ahead.

"Hey!" I call out to him. "You know what's going on?"

He walks up to our car—an older man wearing buffalo print, boots, and a ball cap. "Cops are turning around traffic. There's an accident with a few 18-wheelers up ahead. Looks pretty bad."

"Damn." I look around as vehicles veer off the main highway and cross the grass to turn around. I wave the guy a thank you and slip back into my seat. "Looks like we gotta take a detour."

"Great," Lana rasps.

Mick's already pulling up an app to help us find another direction. "Here." He hands me his phone, and we pull away from the back-to-back traffic.

* * *

"Holly Ridge," Mick sounds out as we pass an old wooden sign on the side of the road covered in Christmas lights.

I've been driving for hours, and a heavy snowfall is making it harder to see the road in front of us. I lean in to see better as Lana messes with the settings on the windshield to help the snow melt faster.

"This isn't looking too good," she whispers, mostly to herself.

Holly Ridge looks like a small, quiet town at the base of a mountain. It's one of those places with tiny shops wafting the smell of warm cinnamon and baked goods. The people we pass walking the streets are bundled up in coats and scarves, and it's clear we're not in Texas anymore. We're also nowhere near Breckenridge yet, with hours still to go.

"What a storybook town," Mick says, sitting up and watching the scenery pass us slowly.

"I think we should stop and get gas," I say.

"Then I'll take us the rest of the way," Lana adds.

I glance at her. "In this weather? Absolutely not."

"Excuse me? Which one of us grew up on the sunny beaches of California while the other one of us practically grew up building igloos?" she protests. "I'm driving us up the mountains."

"No," I say.

"What? You don't think I can?" She crosses her arms like she's done so many times on this trip.

"I think you can do anything I can do and probably do it better," I say.

"Then?"

We pull up to a tiny gas station. There's a brown crown vic with the words *Sheriff* scrawled across the doors parked next to me. A uniformed man tips his hat at us as we park.

"Nothing. I just can't in good conscience let you take on the toughest part of this trip," I continue saying to Lana.

"Because you don't think I can," she says.

I look back at her brother in the back seat.

"Just let her drive, man. You won't hear the end of it," Mick confirms.

Lana extends an empty hand and flexes her fingers, asking for the key.

I reluctantly pull it from the ignition and drop it into her hand. "Fine."

She snatches her hand away before I can change my mind and grabs her sweatshirt and purse before pushing the door open.

"You should probably put on something a little warmer," I say, popping open the trunk to grab my coat from my luggage.

"I'm fine," she says, sashaying past the gawking young sheriff as she slips the hoodie back on.

"You folks staying in town for Christmas?" He asks her.

"Passing through, we're headed up the mountain," Lana says, flashing a sparkling smile that could knock the pants off any man. And I resent the fact that it wasn't directed at me.

"Not tonight you aren't," the Sheriff says with a shake of his head.

I pull my coat out from my bag and slam the trunk before taking the spot next to a now-shivering Lana.

"What do you mean?" she asks.

"Roads are closed. No one's going in or out of town the rest of the night. There's ice on the roads, and we can't have any preventable accidents the day before Christmas Eve."

Mick joins us, throwing on a jacket. "Are you saying we're stuck here?"

The sheriff looks at each of us. "'Fraid, so."

Lana shakes her head. "We don't have any place to stay. Our family is expecting us tonight, and we're already running late due to a detour."

"Sorry, miss, but you'll have to let them know you'll meet them once the storm passes."

"Storm?" We all repeat.

"Mmhmm, big one too, coming in from the Northwest."

"Fucking fantastic," Mick says, zipping up his jacket.

"Are th-there any hotels?" Lana stutters out through chattering teeth.

"Unfortunately, I think the inn is at capacity. The nearest hotel is over thirty miles back the way you came, but like I said, roads are closed." He's rubbing the side of his jaw like he's trying to think of something for us.

"Are we s-supposed to just stay in our car?"

"Do you not have a coat?" I ask the shivering woman next to me.

When she ignores me, I shrug out of my jacket and stretch it over her shoulders. She opens her mouth to say something, but then I rub both sides of her arms to warm her, and she shuts her mouth.

"You know what, let me see if there's something we can do for you nice folks. Why don't you come inside the general store while I make some calls."

"Thank God," Lana says, shifting out of my jacket and handing it back to me as we follow the sheriff through the doors.

Chapter 5
Lana

The general store is warm and cozy, and feels like we've stepped into an 1800s homestead with modern amenities. There's even a cast iron wood stove burning wood in the far corner.

I head there first, ready to defrost my frigid fingers. But also to get away from Trevor as fast as I can. I'm not falling for his little nice guy tactics even for a second. I don't care how cute his dimples are or how warm his gaze on me feels. And that scent. Don't get me started on how this guy smells like the perfect mix of musk and wood... *I need to stop*.

It hasn't even been two months since my wedding day went to shit and I'm already cracking.

I step up to the fire and hold my cold hands out.

I can't let myself be taken advantage of again. *Never again*.

This time, I know better. This time, I'm not a desperate woman trying to get validation from a guy that could never be what I need him to be.

No. Trevor Sincaid won't get access to me. I don't care how much my brother claims to love the guy.

"The sheriff seems to have taken a liking to you," a voice says quietly behind me.

"And you feel the need to mention that to me because...?"

Trevor shrugs, still holding the jacket over his arm that he wrapped me in without asking. It was sweet, but I know better.

"No particular reason, I guess. Just seems to be going out of his way for a group of strangers."

I turn to him. "Maybe if I bat my lashes and shake my ass he'll put us up in a big, fancy cabin. Seems to work for you professional hockey players."

His gentle smile disappears. "I've never shaken my ass to get something. I took my pants off."

I give him a look.

"Besides," he adds gruffly, "I didn't say I liked that he's looking at you."

Wait... what?

Trevor's eyes stay glued to mine and there's a possessive-ness in them that takes me by surprise.

"Woah! You won't believe what the sheriff just got us." My brother walks up to us, swinging a set of keys around his pointer finger breaking our locked gazes.

"Are those the keys to his handcuffs?" I balk at him.

"No," he rustles my hair, and I slap his hand away.

"One of the owners of the inn told him we could stay in his empty cabin just up the hill for the night."

Maybe Trevor was right. It does seem like a lot of trouble for a few strangers just passing through.

"Let me guess, in exchange, he wants Lana's number?" Trevor says, still defensive.

"Nope, but he does want yours."

My eyes shoot back to my brother, and we both say, "What?"

"I mean, your jersey number. Signed. That was his only request. I told him you'd do it, no problem," Vance laughs. "Anything so that we don't have to wait out a snowstorm from my car."

"But I don't have a jersey," Trevor says.

"No need. He's a fan, man. Apparently he has one at the cabin we'll be staying in. It's hanging in one of the guest rooms."

How nice that we'd find ourselves nearly a thousand miles from home and just so happen to run into Trevor's biggest fan.

"But actually now that you mention it, yeah, big bad sheriff dude did low-key ask me for Lana's number."

Trevor gives me an *I told you so* look.

I try to ignore him. "So, where is this cabin?"

"Welp," Vance says. "About that."

* * *

I'm once again engulfed in that scent that is purely Trevor Sincaid. A smell like that should be illegal. It's the kind of fragrance that makes for bad decisions. I realize the effect as I'm grabbing onto his midsection like my life depends on it.

The firm muscles of his stomach tighten at the way I grasp onto him as he speeds over bumps in the snow on the snowmobile.

My brother is riding just next to us. The people of Holly Ridge really are way too trusting to let people they don't know just stay in their cabins and borrow their snowmobiles.

What's next? A visit from the neighbors with a plate of cookies in the morning? Actually that wouldn't be so bad.

The snowmobile hits a bump, and we fly into the air and land with a big thump, my body pushing up against Trevors as my legs hug his thighs in a way that isn't entirely appropriate, but I wasn't about to do this with my brother. Hell no.

Vance stops just before the dark cabin and shuts the ignition off. There aren't any lights for miles, and the cabin looks abandoned and untouched from where we are. Now, it all makes sense.

Trevor parks next to Vance and whistles, saying, "Looks about as festive as your house, little grinch."

I push myself away from him. "You're one to talk."

"I just moved in. What's your excuse?" Trevor says.

Vance quickly dismounts, bounds up the steps to the two-story log cabin, and tries the door. After moments of messing with the lock, he resorts to knocking.

"Don't you have a key?" Trevor calls out to him as he follows him up the steps.

"It's not working," he calls back over his shoulder.

The wind is picking up, and it hasn't stopped snowing since we got into town. It's getting heavier. We weren't able to bring the SUV up the road, so we were only able to bring whatever could fit into backpacks for the night.

Hopefully, *just* for the night.

Tomorrow is Christmas Eve and I can imagine our family all gathered around the warm fire of the cabin in Breckenridge. A picturesque scene glowing behind them in the giant glass wall of the town full of lights and nearby snow-covered mountains. It was the post card that lives in my mind of every Christmas of our childhood.

That's the Christmas I was hoping for. Not getting

detoured, snowed in, and trapped in an abandoned cabin in some small town with my brother and his obnoxious teammate.

An obnoxious teammate whose coat I'm now wearing since I was too aggravated at the sight of him to run back inside and actually grab mine before leaving on this stupid road trip.

Vance finally gets the door open. Inside, we split up in search of light switches. I run my hands over the walls in the dark place and find one, switching it back and forth —nothing.

"Power's out," I announce.

"Ah, shit." Vance pulls out his phone and turns on the flashlight setting. "I'll go outside and look for a breaker box. I'm sure there's one somewhere."

In the brief moment that he opens the door, the howling wind outside blows in more snow than should be allowed. He quickly shuts it behind him leaving Trevor and I alone in the dark.

He turns on his flashlight too and flashes it at me. I cover my eyes as he smiles and moves it around the darkened space.

The light reveals a main living space that has two leather couches covered in an assortment of throw blankets. A wood-burning fireplace. And a small dining table for four. There's a hallway off from the living room that must be where the bedrooms are and a stretch of stairs that lead to the second story.

I pull out my phone to turn my flashlight on as well. But it's dead.

"Hey Sherlock, point your light up there." I motion up the stairs.

"Why?" He says, moving my way. "You scared of ghosts, Lani Banani?"

"My brother's the only one that can call me that and just barely. And no, I'm not scared of anything."

"That's very on-brand for you," he brushes past me and points the light up the steep steps. At the very top is a tiny door that looks like it was created for a leprechaun.

"Creepy," we both say slowly.

"Well, I think we can both agree there's nothing up there for us," he says, stepping further down into the hall and shining the light down revealing three doors. I notice him hesitate.

"Who's scared now?" I smirk, holding my hand out open for him to pass me the phone we're using as a flashlight.

He doesn't think twice before giving it to me.

I huff out a laugh and keep pushing forward. The first door is a bathroom. One that must've been recently remodeled since it has a big glass steam shower next to a very vintage-looking clawfoot bath.

He sticks his face in next to me and whistles. "Fancy," he says. "I call dibs on the shower."

We move on to the other doors. One is a children's room with two little beds—one in pink covers and one in blue. A lamp on a nightstand between the two is in the shape of a star. Quaint and cute.

The second room is my literal worst nightmare. I shut the door behind me so fast before Trevor even has a chance to look in.

"What is it?" he asks, with an eyebrow quirked up in curiosity.

"Just a room, let's go see the kitchen." I attempt to duck around him and draw his attention away.

"Uh uh, gimme that," he reaches for his phone again, and I jump to try to get it back.

"Trevor, no!"

I wrestle it back out of his hands, and he catches me by the waist and swings me back against the wall, trapping me between his arms.

"Give me my phone, Lana," his voice sounds like a threat, but I know better. The little curve at the corner of his lip gives away his playfulness.

"No," I say again, trapping the phone behind my back. In a panic, I slip it into my pants.

His eyes widen. "Did you just stick my phone in your ass crack?"

The way he says *ass crack* filled with so much disbelief makes me burst out into a laugh that makes me bend forward just enough that he reaches behind me and slips his hand into the waistband of my jeans.

"Get your hand away from my ass!" I bark out with a laugh, twisting away from him.

"No, *you* get my phone out of your ass. You weirdo!" He twists me around, and now my back is to him. I quickly press into him so he can't reach between us and retrieve his precious phone. And as soon as I do, I'm able to feel him hard and excited behind me.

Good God. What is this man packing?

Before the thought completely overtakes me, he tickles the area beneath my ribs, which is the most ticklish spot on my body. I cry out for him to stop and pull away from him, just as he shoves his hand down my pants and pulls out his phone.

"What is wrong with you?" He chuckles, holding the phone away from my grasp. "You don't want me to see what's in this room that much?"

Anne Martin

I'm still holding the side of my body where his fingers dug into me and made me lose all control just moments before. "Don't," I breathe out as he puts his hand on the door handle.

He grins triumphantly and pushes the door open. The second he does, the lights come on illuminating the entire house, but especially this space in such a way that it feels like a special middle finger from the entire universe to me.

Heatwave merch is everywhere. And when I say everywhere, I mean *everywhere,* from the bedspread with the signature flaming puck logo with a giant H to the jerseys lining the wall of every player in this season's starting lineup. Orange and yellow are the colors accenting the black in the space.

The owner of this cabin isn't just a fan of the Houston Heatwave; he might just be their number one fan.

Which is excellent... just freakin' fantastic.

Trevor spots his number two jersey among the others. Balinger, O'Connor, Ferguson, Hicks (who doesn't even play for them anymore, but hey), Landry, and of course...

"Would you look at that?" he says with a grin so incorrigible I might slap it off his face. "That must be the jersey he wants me to sign."

All the others already sport his teammate's signatures.

The front door slams, and my brother stomps his feet at the entrance before his heavy footsteps meet us at the end of the hall.

"Well, we got pow—Woah," Vance says, mouth agape as he enters the space.

"There's more Heatwave merch here than at the store at Space City Arena." Vance points to the wall of jerseys. "They forgot the best player, though."

I shove him in the side. "Alright, you two narcissists, let's figure out what the hell we're going to eat tonight."

I turn the light off and head to the kitchen. And I can hear them playing rock, paper, scissors over who gets the Heatwave room.

"Gah! Best two out of three," Trevor offers.

"Nope, enjoy the toddler bed," my brother says to him.

Now that the house is completely illuminated I'm able to really take in its charm. It's warm like a cute family might stay here every once in a while, but not overly decorated that it feels gaudy. The typical things you'd find in a mountain cabin occupy the space. Hand-carved furniture, wool blankets, oil paintings of mountainous scenes, and candles. Lots of candles everywhere. Probably due to the fact that they lose power a lot out here as we just witnessed.

Trevor opens a cabinet in the kitchen. "They have a lot of canned goods." He opens another. "Like, a lot of canned foods."

Vance grabs one from the open cabinet. "Peaches, corn, peas... we can make quite a canned food casserole."

I make a heaving sound.

"Oh, hush. You love my cooking."

"Excuse me?" I laugh out. "Your cooking? Since when do you cook?"

"Excuse me," my brother mimics me. "But I've cooked ever since I realized that girls are more attracted to Chef Daddy than a hockey one."

"A Chef Daddy?" Trevor snorts to himself, still searching cabinets and then opens the fridge—empty. But in the freezer, he sees something that makes him smile.

"You guys..." he pulls it out and shakes the chilled bottle at us.

"Vodka? I don't know, man," my brother hesitates.

"Are you pro players not allowed to drink vodka?" I ask him, leaning against the small island in the middle of the kitchen; I'm rubbing my arms because it's still so cold in this house.

"Our training staff aren't too keen on us partaking in alcoholic beverages during the season," Vance clarifies.

"But lucky for us," Trevor opens the lid and downs a big gulp. "None of them are here right now."

He passes the open bottle to my brother, who stares at it a moment too long. I roll my eyes and grab the bottle, bringing the cold glass to my lips and taking an extra strong pull of it.

If I'm going to be stranded in a cabin in the middle of nowhere just before Christmas with two men... then I'll take all the alcohol I can get.

"Lana MacDonald," Trevor says in an appreciative voice. "Didn't think you had it in you."

I take a second giant gulp before handing him the bottle.

"Well, while my brother whips us up some canned dinner, I'm going to go chop us up some wood for the fire," I say.

Both guys look at me like I just lost my mind.

"You're not going out there," Vance says. "Trust me, the wind alone will blow you down the mountain we just rode up."

"Don't be ridiculous. I'll be fine. I've been in worse." I zip Trevor's coat up to my neck and pull on the hoodie.

Trevor stares at me for a second before taking another pull of vodka, setting it on the counter, and turning to Vance.

"Give me your coat." He holds a hand out, waiting for him.

"My coat? As in the one I'm currently wearing so as not to die of frostbite?"

"Yes, that coat. I'm going with her."

"No, you're not," I protest.

Vance looks at him but ultimately gives in and shrugs out of his giant coat. Trevor slips it on, zips it up, and turns to me. "The lady wants firewood, so let's chop some firewood."

"I don't need your help," I say to him, turning to exit the back of the house.

"Well, if the winds are going to blow you down the mountain, I'd at least like to watch. Make sure they finish the job."

I glower at him, and he grins at me.

I pull the coat hoodie closer around my face and brace for the cold wind before turning back to Trevor.

"Just try to keep up."

Chapter 6
Trevor

L ana is surprisingly gifted at wielding an axe. A detail I don't plan on forgetting anytime soon considering how much she doesn't like me.

Though I'm pretty sure she didn't miss the fact that I am very attracted to her—the raging bulge in my pants earlier was proof of that. I was hoping she wouldn't notice, but come on—her ass was literally rubbing against me. What am I supposed to do... not get turned on?

She stabilizes a piece of wood against the trunk and positions the axe just above her head. In one swift movement, she's able to split the wood in two.

I shudder at the thought of what she could do with that axe if she knew I was thinking about her pressed up against me.

"Alright, Woody Woodpecker. Let me have a go, would you? Show you how a real man chops wood."

She gives me a look that says, *I'd like to see you try,* but reluctantly hands me the axe.

"Don't hurt yourself," she says coldly.

"Aww, you do care."

"No, it would just be a real inconvenience to have to bury you up here in this frozen tundra. Although, I'm sure the wolves wouldn't mind having a Christmas feast."

"You're a real charmer, you know that, Lana MacDonald." I line up a piece of wood and pull the axe over my head.

"Too high," she observes. I'm about to slam it down, but her remark makes me pause.

"What?"

"Your grip. It needs to be a little lower," she says, watching me.

I move my hand on the grip and look at her for approval.

"Perfect. Now, instead of aiming for the wood on the trunk, aim for the one in your pants, and don't ever let me see that again."

It takes me a second to register what she's saying but when I do I turn to look at her. "Wait... is my biggest anti-fan standing in sub-zero weather and thinking about my wood?" I can't even try to hide the smile.

Lana noticed. And not only did she notice. She's still thinking about it. Which makes me... an idiot. Have I learned nothing? Just because a woman says something doesn't mean it has the same meaning to me as it does to her.

"Do you always get hard during tickle fights?" she cocks her head at me.

"Do you want to test your theory?"

I slam the axe down onto the wood. It doesn't quite snap in two. I try again. Still no luck.

Okay, clearly I'm not a lumberjack. Third times a charm and when it finally cracks open for me, I turn to look at Lana who's laughing to herself and shaking her head.

"That the best you can do, stud?"

I shoot her a glare. "You haven't seen nothing yet."

I toss the wood into the small pile we're accumulating and grab another piece to chop.

This time, instead of coaching me from afar, Lana closes the distance between us and puts her hands over mine on the axe, helping me to adjust my hold.

"Like that," she instructs into my ear. Her voice is low and raspy, and it does something to me, despite the ridiculously cold weather.

She takes a step back, and this time, in one fell swoop, I'm able to split the wood in two.

I huff out a laugh. "You're a good coach."

"It's kind of what I do, Sincaid."

She adds the wood to the growing pile, lines up another and takes the axe back. Destroying two more pieces of wood.

"Where'd you learn to be a lumberjack?" I ask, grabbing some of the wood into my arms.

"My dad," she says, slamming the axe onto the trunk and joining me in picking up the pieces.

I watch her as she moves. Strong, solid movements. She's the kind of woman that seems to be confident in anything that she does.

And I find that to be really fucking hot.

"Didn't realize professional lumberjacks still existed."

"They mostly use equipment and chainsaws now, but growing up our dad ran a Christmas tree farm out near Ottawa."

I pause what I'm doing.

"A Christmas tree farm?" I ask, probably a little too incredulously.

"Yes," she says eyeing me. "Why?"

"It's just interesting... I'm picturing grouchy little Lana.

The grinch of the MacDonald family learning to chop down trees to bring Christmas joy to all the little girls and boys just sounds... I don't know, funny."

"I am not the family grinch."

"It's okay, Lana. Every family has one. For mine, it's my oldest brother Harlan. I think he'd rather skip the whole Thanksgiving to Christmas season altogether if he could."

"I love Christmas, Sincaid."

I blow air through my lips, "Sure, why don't you prove it then?"

"I don't need to prove anything to you." She puts a hand up to her hip.

"Because you're a little Christmas grinch?"

She scoffs. I gotta admit, I like ruffling her feathers. It's fun.

I turn, about to pick up another piece of wood to chop when something whizzes past my face. At first, I think it's a bird. But as I turn to see the direction it came from a burst of ice cold snow hits me square in the face.

As it drips off, I see Lana, keeled over and laughing in such a way that I almost can't be mad that she just hit me in the face.

"Oh, you think that's funny? " I say, wiping the slush off my face.

She giggles and it's the cutest fucking thing I've ever heard. Of course, it is. Of course I find the giggle of the most menacing human on earth to be the one thing that does me out.

I reach down to roll up a snowball and I as I do she hits me with three more.

"Jesus, woman. How many arms do you have?" I launch my flimsy excuse for a snowball at her but she's already running away.

"La-na," I call out behind her. "You want to start a war? Then stay and fight."

She doesn't stop, instead she jumps up pulling an icicle from a branch as she runs under it and launches it at me. I'm now full-on chasing her into the woods as the icicle zings past me.

"I almost lost an eye!" I yell up to her.

"An eye patch might actually fix your face," she calls back, huffing to catch air in her lungs.

"I hope you run better than you can throw an icicle because when I catch you," I threaten. "It's over."

Another snowball gets tossed in my direction. It's like she's making them as she's running which is just insane. Maybe she has the forest animals helping her out. I'm right on her tail as we break past the tree line and into a clearing, where she jumps over a fallen log but trips up and lands right in the snow with a yelp.

I got her now.

I jump the log and land right over her as she's kicking up snow and trying to get away.

I pull her legs and slide her to me, using my hips to pin her down as I lean forward and take both her wrists into one hand, pinning her arms above her head.

She writhes under me. And the motion mixed with the adrenaline has me getting excited in a way neither one of us can deny.

Lana breathes heavily, trying to escape from my grip.

"Uh-uh," I say. "An eye for an eye." I dig my free hand into the snow next to her hip and grab a handful.

"Let. Me. Go!" She fights with each word.

"Not until I get my payback," I say, squeezing the snow into a tight fist and letting it slightly melt into a piece of ice in my grip.

Lana looks at my hand, confusion written all over her face.

I take the ice and run it down the side of her face. She gasps and keeps trying to buck me off of her, but I keep trailing it down the side of her neck.

She stops moving and instead just swallows, waiting to see what I'll do next.

"You want to play, little grinch?" I whisper to her. "I'll play."

I dip the piece of ice into her jacket, and she squeals as it gets lost in her shirt.

This time I let her buck me off her, and I land on my back in the snow next to her, laughing as she jumps to her feet and bounces up and down to get the piece of ice out of her shirt.

"You son of a—"

"Hey!" The back door to the cabin swings open. I can see Mick appear in the distance. "Did you losers leave me to fend for myself?"

I push myself up just as Lana finishes twisting every which way to get the ice out of her shirt. It's a much smaller piece when it falls to the snow beneath her which tells me it mostly melted against her skin.

"Come on, little grinch," I brush past her and start making my way back toward the cabin.

"Oh, you're not getting off that easy," Lana says, walking faster and leaving me behind.

I pick up my pace so that I'm right next to her. But she moves even faster, now in a jog.

I'm not used to the elevation out here, so it doesn't take much for me to start huffing and puffing. And she notices it right away.

"What's the matter, stud? Can't keep up?" The teasing

in her eyes only works to fuel my fire. I take a deep breath and try to keep my calm.

"Guys?!" Mick calls again.

We're running next to each other now, and just as we make it past the trees and tumble into the chopping area, Mick finally sees us.

"What the hell were you two doing? Hunting for dinner?" He wraps a scarf closer to his face.

"Just a little friendly competition," I huff out.

"What's wrong with him?" He asks his sister, who just looks at me and shrugs.

"Weak lungs?"

I shoot her a glare.

"Well, I got some news. Want the good or the bad first?"

"Whichever it is, can we hear it inside?" I say, now shivering from the sweat Lana has induced.

Mick holds the back door open for us to walk through and Lana and I both take a step in simultaneously, bumping our shoulders together as we both try to squeeze through.

Mick gives us both a shove, and we nearly fall all over each other.

"Just lay it on us," Lana tells her brother, that coldness back in her voice.

"Bad news is, the storm's not expected to let up until Christmas night," Mick announces as he shuts the door to keep the wind from blowing in snow.

"What? H-how do you know that?" Lana says in a panic.

"I found a crank radio in the attic, and yeah... it's a big one."

Shit. That means we're stuck here. I look at Lana, who looks like someone just told her Santa isn't real.

"But the good news is... they have Christmas decorations up there!" Mick offers.

"Are you serious right now? We're stuck here for Christmas?" Lana crosses her arms over her chest. "You're sure?"

"Pretty damn sure," Mick says, grabbing some gloves off the kitchen counter. "Which means we're going to need more than just canned goods to get us through the next two days."

"We don't have the car," Lana says, turning to him.

"No, but we have the snowmobile. I can ride down, get some more supplies, and see if the owner will let us stay an extra night. Plus, there's no cell service up here. I need to see if maybe by getting closer to some wifi, I'll be able to reach mom and dad and let them know where we are."

"No cell service?" Lana falls onto the couch, looking defeated. "Awesome. There goes our Christmas."

"We'll make the most of it. I promise," Mick says. He grabs the goggles he used to ride on the snowmobile.

"You can't go out there alone," Lana says.

"Well, I'm not letting you go out there, and I'm not letting you stay here alone, so..."

"I'll go get the supplies," I offer.

Mick looks at me. "Do you even know what kind of supplies to get, Cali boy?"

"Really, Mick? We're not camping out in the woods. What kind of stuff would we need to wait out a snowstorm?"

"Yeah... I'm not leaving our survival up to you," Mick says.

"Thank God," Lana adds under her breath.

"You two get the fire going. If I'm not back in a few hours, just assume wolves ate me and move on with your lives."

"He's so dramatic," Lana says.

"Fuck dude," I say.

He laughs. "I'm kidding. I'll be back. Oh, and maybe throw up some of those decorations from the attic. Just because we're stuck here doesn't mean we have to give up on the holidays entirely."

Mick waves and disappears into the dark forest on the snowmobile. When the tail lights are at a far enough distance, I turn to Lana, who is stacking the firewood in the fireplace.

"Looks like it's just you and me, little grinch."

"Great, just so we get this out in the open... I'm not sleeping with you." She doesn't even bother looking my way.

"Great, just so we get it out in the open... I wasn't *planning* on sleeping with you."

"Good," she says. "Because neither was I."

"Even though you thought about it," I point out.

"No, I didn't."

"Yes, you had to think about it in order to tell me that. So you did at least consider it."

"And I concluded that I won't."

"Right, but you admit you thought about it. Even though nobody asked."

"Why are you this insufferable?"

"Because Lana, like a rock trapped inside your shoe, I am impossible to ignore. Which is why the second your brother walked out the door, you thought about sleeping with me." I give her a smirk.

"*Not* sleeping with you," she corrects me.

"Case in point."

"You're not going to win this," she states.

"Oh, I'm going to win this. Because of the two of us here,

who's the professional Lana, and who's the one who has to resort to coaching?"

She gets up from the couch and stalks over to the back door.

"I'm going to pretend I didn't just hear you say that."

Jackpot. I got her.

"Those who can't do... teach," I say with a shrug.

She opened the door, but the moment the words leave my lips she slams it shut and walks over to me. With a shove at the corner of my shoulder she says, "I'm not resorting to coaching. I *chose* coaching, you dick. Because guys like you only know how to help yourselves and would never reach a hand back to guide a young girl who wants a seat at your table. So I'm coaching to do that and to make sure they know exactly how to put up with assholes in their field."

"So I'm an asshole. I'm a dick. All because I'm a professional in sports."

"Professional is a stretch," she scoffs.

I stand there staring at her.

"I wonder what would happen if you'd stop considering me the enemy just because I'm a man... and would treat me like an equal."

"Are you kidding me right now? An equal? Am I an equal to you?"

"No," I say sternly.

"Wooow. See? And you wonder why I hate you."

"No," I say stepping closer to her, closing the distance between us. "I'm not your equal. You are by far more intelligent. More skilled. And most definitely *way* more sexy," I say, lowering my voice as I stand face-to-face with her.

"Don't do that," she says in a near whisper.

"Do what?" I cock my head at her.

"Don't try to win me over."

I take a step closer to her and notice how her chest rapidly rises and falls.

"I'm not trying anything," I say. "I'm just telling you the truth. I think you got me all wrong, little grinch. I'm not who you think I am."

"And who's that?" she asks, eyeing me suspiciously.

"I'm not whoever hurt you. I'm not the one who left you. I'm just Trevor. And I know we just met, but I already know —I'm your biggest fan."

"You just insulted me, and now you're saying this. I don't need you to be my biggest fan; I need you to just stay away," she nearly barks at me.

Then she sidesteps me and leaves out the back door, shutting it abruptly behind her and making the pictures on the walls shake.

Well, that went very well.

Normally I'd cut my loses and take a hint... but there's something about my teammate's sister that makes me want to try harder.

I'm going to break her. I'm going to have her begging for me.

And I'll be a happy man if it's the only thing I get for Christmas.

The game is on.

Chapter 7
Lana

I toss another piece of wood into the stoked fire. I love the smell of burning wood, it brings me right back to the cold Christmas winters back in Canada growing up.

Snow falls. Cozy fires. Hot chocolate. Christmas lights.

I look around the near empty living room. Trevor is nowhere in sight. I told him to stay away, and except for bringing down a small tree for me to flock, it seems like he's doing just that.

Good. I'm glad he finally took a hint. Because I can't be around him without completely losing my mind, apparently. Nobody should smell that good. Nobody should *feel* that good pressed against me.

And now I find myself dwelling on the fact that Trevor Sincaid might actually be one of the most attractive humans I've ever been around. Which makes me dislike him even more.

He's not the kind of guy I'd typically be attracted to. I tend to go for a less playful type. More serious. More goal-oriented. Someone who knows what he wants in life.

My ex, basically.

But Trevor has this way about him. He's cool. Unbothered. Everything seems like a game to him.

There's a thump against the floor above me followed by a loud grunt. And it sounds like he just stubbed his toe. I grab the stoker and push around the firewood, watching the fire build.

There's another loud thump.

What the hell is he doing up there?

Annoyed, I make my way down the hallway. "Trevor?"

I don't hear anything.

Did he die?

"Trevor?" I call out again.

Another loud thump.

Nope, still alive.

I make my way up the small staircase that leads up to the creepy door of the attic. The light at the top is dim but enough for me to get a good view of him without him seeing me.

He has a pair of headphones sitting on top of his head and he's humming to something he's listening to as he shuffles some boxes around. All of which would be completely acceptable except that he's not wearing a shirt.

I watch as he takes a box down from a stack, his muscles coiling as he reaches overhead. He has a nice back—strong, toned and it's adorned by a giant tattoo scrawled across his skin.

I watch as he moves and I finally hear the words to the song he's singing.

Stargazing. Ugh. Way to ruin a moment. I move to go downstairs but I hear my name.

I turn just as I watch him take his headphones off.

"Were you just watching me, little grinch?"

"I thought you died," I blurt out.

He chuckles. "What?"

"The noise... I thought you died."

"Sorry to disappoint. Just looking for those damn decorations your brother was talking about. Whoever lives here doesn't believe in labels and I'm starting to think he just sent me on a wild goose chase."

I step through the tiny door, wondering how a guy of Trevor's stature—and especially my brothers—is even able to get through it.

"It can't be that hard." I eye the boxes he's already moved, then back to him. "Aren't you cold?"

He looks down at his abs—glistening like he just got done working out—then looks back at me.

"Does my half-naked body offend you, little grinch?"

"No," I scoff.

"Because apparently, my shirtless self doth offend the female species."

"It's very... shiny," I observe.

A small grin pulls at the corner of his lips and his dimple pulses. "Shiny?"

I toss my hand in his direction. "Mick will be here any minute. He'll wonder what the heck we've been doing all this time if he doesn't see decorations."

I pull down another box and open it—just books.

"Oh, right, and we wouldn't want him to think we were doing anything freaky."

I give him a look. "I don't think anyone would accuse you of being a freak," I say.

"How would you know, Lana? How would you know I'm not a closet freak?"

"Are you?" I ask him.

He seems to like that I'm digging because his eyes light up.

"Wouldn't you like to know, little grinch?"

"I wouldn't, actually."

"When was the last time you had sex?" he asks nonchalantly. I drop the book in my hand, and it falls back into the box.

"Excuse me? That's none of your business."

He lowers down another box from the shelves and pushes it toward me.

"So you can ask me if I'm a freak, but I'm not allowed to ask you when's the last time you got freaky?" He grunts as he shoves the box closer to me.

I sigh. "You first."

He straightens and places his hands on his hips. The pants he's wearing sit low enough on them to give me a good view of the 'v' shape of his muscles. It takes everything in me to pull my eyes away.

"I guess it's been... over a year? Maybe more." He goes back to moving boxes.

I cough on nothing. "Over a year?!"

He looks at me and shrugs.

"That can't be right," I say, pulling the box he brought to open closer to me—this one contains extra bedding.

"Why? Because it would go against everything you believe about me being a slutty hockey player?"

My eyes lock with his. "Maybe."

"I told you I'm not who you think I am. Your turn," he says.

I get flashes of that last night with my ex-fiance. I wouldn't have suspected a thing. I would've married him. And I would've been an idiot.

"I... can't remember," I lie.

"That bad, huh?"

"No, it was adequate."

He turns to look at me. "Adequate—sounds like the epitome of romance. I guess we can assume "*freak*" isn't included in your bio either."

I scoff, "It wasn't for lack of trying."

He pushes another box around and then turns to watch me.

"Oh yeah? What's the freakiest thing you've done, little grinch?"

I know what he's doing. He's baiting me. "I'm not about to tell you that."

Leaning on a stack of boxes, he slides his hands into his pocket.

"Because you're scared I'll like what I hear?"

My eyes flick to his. I'd be lying if I didn't admit that his presence does something to me.

I lick my lips. "I think my imagination is freakier than I am in real life."

He straightens. "Is that right? Then what's something you've thought about, Lana?"

My heart starts to race. Nobody's ever asked me questions like this before. I hardly know him, but the way he watches me, head cocked and ready to hear what I have to say, it feels nice.

"Forget it; you'll think I'm crazy."

He laughs. "Sorry to disappoint you yet again, but I already think you're crazy."

I give him a look.

"You sat on the hood of your car to keep it from getting towed," he reminds me.

"Ha! Yeah, speaking of that–"

He puts a hand up. "I'm paying for you to get it back. I already talked to John."

"As you should!"

He's still watching me. "Now, about those fantasies."

"I want to be chased and tied up," I blurt out. I feel my cheeks heating at the admission.

Trevor's lips part as he takes in a breath. "Chased... and tied up," he repeats thoughtfully.

"I told you I'd sound crazy."

He walks over to me, where I'm seated on the heels of my feet on the ground. And reaches for my chin so that I'm looking up at him. He bends slightly.

"Like earlier... in the snow?"

I give a slight nod. Remembering how good it felt. The adrenaline coursing through my veins, fleeing from danger and then getting caught—his body pressed against mine. I haven't felt that thrill in so long.

"And then what?" he asks lowly. "What would you want to happen to you once you're tied up?"

I try to swallow, but it feels even more exaggerated because of the way he's holding my chin.

"I-I haven't thought that far..." I say.

Trevor chuckles deep in his chest. "Oh yes, you have, little grinch. Say it. What would you want to happen if you've been chased and tied up?"

His eyes hold my gaze so intently I feel like my insides are about to combust. I don't talk like this. I don't admit these things to men.

"I'll help you out," he says, dropping his hand from my chin and moving behind me. He squats, and I can feel his breath behind my ear as he whispers. "Would you want to be choked?... Spanked?... Fucked?" he says.

My eyes widen, and I swallow hard and croak out a weak, "Yes."

Still behind me, his hand grabs a hold of my throat. He doesn't choke me. He just puts a light pressure on it and forces me to look at him.

"You, little grinch... are quite the freak then." He grins, his eyes bouncing across my features. He's close enough to kiss.

The front door opens downstairs and slams. "Honey, I'm home," my brother announces. "And it's cold as shit out there."

I scramble to my feet, nearly pushing Trevor down the stairs as I do.

"Where are you guys?" Vance asks, down the hall.

"Upstairs," I say, a little too squeaky for my liking. I clear my throat, "We found the decorations."

I look at Trevor who's slowly rising to his feet and casually sliding his hands back into his pocket, heated eyes watching me.

"Put your shirt on!" I whisper-yell to him.

He looks down at his body. His pants are tented in such a way that he wouldn't be able to deny what was just happening up here. Then he looks back at me.

"I think I'll stay like this. But thanks."

"Oh my god," I say, grabbing some ornaments from a box and heading down the stairs.

I need to get it together. This is Trevor Sincaid. My brother's teammate and friend. The neighbor that I can't stand. And the man who just got me to admit that I might be a little sick in the head when it comes to the intimacy department.

Oh my god! Did I really just admit those things to him?

What if he tells Vance? Or the rest of his team? What if he uses it against me, and I lose my job?

Shit. I shouldn't ever have fallen for his stupid trap.

I nearly run into my brother once I get down the steep steps.

"Hey!" I laugh nervously.

"Hey," he says, looking behind me suspiciously. "You good?"

"Yep!" I hold up the small ornament box. "Just gonna go... you know, decorate."

"Right," he says. "I got some stuff for soup tonight and dinner tomorrow."

"Awesome, can't wait." I push past him and nearly stumble into the living room.

"I'm just gonna take a quick shower and try to thaw out," Vance calls out to me.

I'm already hanging ornaments on the tree when I hear him close a door down the hall.

Phew, that was close. What would've happened up there if Vance hadn't returned just now.

What kind of things would Trevor and I be getting into?

The thought barely has time to formulate when I hear footsteps coming up behind me. A box is dropped beside me.

"Don't you think we should start with the lights?" Trevor says.

"Oh... yeah, I guess that would make sense."

He reaches into the box and pulls out a string of lights, unrolling them. "We should test them out first. Make sure they work."

"Mmhmm," I hum back.

"What's wrong, Lana? You seem a little nervous," he eyes me as he continues to unroll the string of lights.

"I'm not. I'm fine." Ah shit. I did it again. I'm totally *not* fine. I'm currently imagining him using those lights to do things with me, and I really, really shouldn't.

He watches me closely and hands me the end of the string. "Here hold this while I plug them in."

I take the lights, and his hand brushes against mine, briefly, but enough to send a shiver up my arm.

I'm way too on edge.

Why did I have to get so vulnerable with him? I wish I could just take it all back.

Trevor, who still hasn't put on a shirt, bends down and sticks the plug into the socket. The lights blink to life and all the colors make the space instantly feel like the holidays.

"They work," he says.

"They do. Listen," I look back to make sure my brother isn't around. "About what I said up there. Can we just keep that between the two of us? It's not something I really want people to know. You know?"

Trevor licks his lips and walks over to me. He takes the lights in my hand and in one swift motion, takes my wrists and winds the string around them, creating a quick knot with them.

"What are you doing?" I breathe out.

"Testing the tie,", he pulls it toward him. Then he takes one hand, backs me up against the wall next to the fireplace, and tugs the lights so that my hands go up over my head, exposing me to him.

"You're telling me you don't want people to know that you liked to get fucked well, little grinch?"

His hips pin me against the wall, and as he does, I feel his erection right on my stomach. Hard and thick as he watches my breath rising and falling. I try to pull my arms down, but he tightens his grip.

"You want to be tied up, you naughty girl. Admit that you like this. Admit that you want more," he teases, whispering against my ear.

"No," I breathe out.

"No, you won't admit it? Or no, you don't want it?"

I gulp. "I won't admit it."

A grin spreads across his face. "But you already did, little grinch."

He's looking down at me, his eyes flicking from my eyes to my lips, then back up.

I do like this. I like it so much. Nobody's ever taken liberties like this... but then again, nobody's ever just asked.

But Trevor did.

His chest is on mine and I'm sure he can feel my nipples hardening through my shirt.

He leans in and whispers against my lips. "Don't play coy now, Lana. I can feel your heart beating against my chest. You love this." He tugs harder and and I gasp against his lips. I squeeze my thighs together, craving friction. Wishing he'd press himself into me more.

"How wet are you right now, little grinch?"

"I'm not," I say, defiantly.

He chuckles, taking his free hand and bringing it to my waistband. He slips his hand down between my legs and when he finds the moisture pooling there he whispers, "Liar."

I gulp, shutting my eyes as he does the thing I want. He presses his body against me, pinning me into the wall. I'm helpless against the Christmas lights restraining my hands above my head as he takes the slickness in his hand and moves it in a delicious circle against my clit.

I shutter, opening my eyes to see his hungry on me. His lips part and he slowly lifts his glistening middle finger to his mouth, his lips wrapping around as he sucks on it and licks the taste of me right off.

Oh my god.

"You taste... sinful, Lana. Wanna taste?"

I gulp giving him a small nod and before I can say anything his lips are on mine and he takes me in a dizzying kiss. His tongue parts my lips, meeting mine. And I want nothing more than for him to just take me right here, right now with the fire roaring next to us.

But the bathroom door opens down the hall. Our lips break apart and he lets go of his hold on my wrists.

In no rush at all, Trevor walks to the kitchen and starts unloading the groceries from the two bags on the island just as Vance walks in.

Nearly busted... again. But this time, I'm in a much more compromising position.

Vance takes one look at me, my wrists wrapped up in the string lights, and laughs. "What the hell is wrong with you?"

My thoughts exactly... *what the hell is wrong with me?*

"Uh," I look down at the lights twisted around my wrist. "I got a little tied up," I say, holding up the tangle.

"Better you do it than me, tangled lights are a bitch," Vance says, going to the kitchen to help Trevor.

Trevor looks over at me with a smirk and I roll my eyes, trying to untie myself.

"Let me," Trevor says, coming back over to me, and as he does my heartbeat picks up its pace.

He reaches for my wrists and unties the lights quickly.

"Got yourself into a little mess there, didn't you, little grinch?" he says playfully.

"You know," Vance says from the kitchen. "I thought for

sure I'd come home to Lana digging up a grave in the backyard, but I didn't expect to see this."

Trevor and I both glance at each other quickly.

"A nice fire going, a tree about to be decorated, you two... being cordial. It's nice," Vance says. "It makes Christmas trapped in a random cabin in a random town just a little bit better."

Right... *cordial.* That's what's happening between his teammate and I. We're being cordial.

"Did you find out if we can stay the extra day?" Trevor says, backing away from me and stringing the lights on the tree.

"I did. And got a hold of mom and pops too."

"What'd they say?" I ask him.

"They're sad for us to miss Christmas with them, but they'd rather we be safe." Vance grabs a pot from one of the cabinets. "We should play some music."

"Maybe have some drinks?" Trevor says, swishing the bottle of vodka from earlier around.

"Fine," Vance says grabbing it and taking a swig. "One drink."

Chapter 8
Trevor

"Y ou might be faster than me, but I'm bigger," Mick slurs at me as Lana and I drag him down the hall to his bed.

"Trust me, I know," I tell him, hitching him up as he stumbles. "Much bigger."

"I thought you said you'd have one drink," Lana chastises him.

"I don't drink, Lana. It's been a while," Mick slurs again.

We make it to the Heatwave room and dump him onto the bed watching him fall like a giant tree getting chopped down.

Lana and I both stare at him.

"Should we just leave him like that?"

She shakes her head, "Help me at least get his head near the pillow."

She climbs onto the bed and drags him by the arms while I push him by the feet.

He mumbles something into the pillow.

"What?"

He tosses himself around until he's on his back. "Don't hurt her."

Lana scrunches her face. "Don't hurt who?"

"I'm talking to him." He points to me. "Don't hurt my sister. She's one of the good ones, and I don't want to have to kill you too."

He then drops his arm over his face and starts to snore. Lana slides off the bed and heads for the door.

"Kill me too?" I whisper after her.

When we're back in the hall, she turns to me. "It's a long story, and I need to shower."

The thought of her with no clothes on already has me way too excited for my own good.

"Tell you what," I say, taking her by the hips and tugging her to me. "Why don't you go shower... and meet me out by the fire. I'll have something waiting for you."

"If it's you gift wrapped under the tree, I think I'll pass," she says.

"Damn it. Okay, I'll come up with something."

She smiles and places a hand on my chest, pushing me away. "Better be good."

"Oh, you're going to fucking melt, Ice Queen."

With one final once-over she disappears into the room and I make my way into the kitchen to make the best damn hot cocoa anyone has ever tasted.

At least, I'll try. Luckily the owners have baking goods in stock, and Mick bought milk.

"Don't hurt her," I scoff, mixing in vanilla and cinnamon to give it that signature "Sincaid" flavor.

I wouldn't hurt, Lana. I just want to show her that being stuck in a cabin with me just might be the best thing to happen to her.

At least, it definitely is the best thing to happen to me.

The woman is a masterpiece. A literal dream and after just one taste, I can't stop thinking of her.

The cocoa now hot, I turn the stove off and pour two mugs. Lana and I didn't get drunk like her brother, but just tipsy enough to forget our feud... for now at least. But hopefully, for good. Because I would love nothing more than to show her what being taken care of can really feel like.

Fuck that guy in the photos. If he did what I think he did, he doesn't deserve to ever breathe the same air as her if I have anything to do with it.

The bathroom door opens, and Lana steps out in a little silk pajama top and shorts ensemble. The cabin is still pretty cold except for the area near the fire. She smells like flowers, soft and sensual, as she approaches me, tugging her tight curls out of a bun and shaking them out.

So beautiful. The second she gets to me, I hand her a mug. "Hey," I say.

"Hey," she says back, taking a sip of the hot liquid. Her eyes widen and she looks at me. "Wow, what did you put in this?"

"Crack," I say matter-of-factly, guiding her to the couch with my hand on the small of her back.

She huffs out a laugh, the mug still to her lips ready for another sip.

"It's my mom's recipe," I admit, as we both take a seat next to each other. The smooth skin of her thigh brushing against my sweatpants.

"My mom would love this recipe."

"Really, well I can't wait to make it for her."

Something twists in her face. It's subtle, but she masks it by taking another sip.

"What?"

She sighs before turning to me.

"I just got out of a relationship, Trevor."

At least she called me by my first name. That's a relief.

"Okay... so what? I can't meet your parents. You do know that's exactly what I was going to do before this storm hit, right?"

"Yeah, but as my brother's friend."

"And I'm still that."

She looks at me but doesn't say anything.

"What is it, little grinch? Are you scared that you no longer hate me because you like the way I kiss you too much?"

My eyes flick to her lips as she sucks in her bottom lip and I'm flooded with the memory of the taste of her earlier.

"You and I both know you didn't *just* kiss me," she says lowly.

"No, I didn't." I set my mug on the little table next to the couch and turn to her. "And if your brother hadn't walked in on us, I would've been able to do a whole lot more."

She gulps but doesn't move. I take the mug from her and place it next to mine on the table.

"Unless," I say. "You wanted me to stop." I move in closer, and she backs into the armrest of the sofa, leaning back.

"I didn't want you to stop," she whispers. "I... don't want you to stop."

I'm over her now, and I grab her by the knees and pull her down under me so that our faces meet.

"Is that so?"

Her eyes twinkle with mischief and it takes everything in me not to just rip the buttons of her top off so I can kiss her everywhere she deserves to be kissed.

She reaches for my neck and pulls me to her, our lips

finding each other again. This time, the kiss is slow and sensual and she takes her time kissing me. But then out of nowhere, she breaks our kiss.

"I need to tell you something."

Uh-uh. Here it is. I knew there would a be but somewhere.

"You're saving yourself for marriage?" I ask her.

Her laugh rolls through her chest and out her nose. "No, it's not that."

"Then?" I ask, cocking my head to the side.

"I... we can't do anything outside of here."

"What do you mean?"

"I mean, you and I... whatever this is. It stays here."

"And what is this?" I ask her.

If you ask me, this is two people realizing there might be something more than just a rivalry. But to her...

"It's just lust."

"Lust," I say.

"I want you. And you want me. But it's just physical."

Just physical because how could she ever want a stupid jock who thinks with his cock. I see.

"Ok, little grinch. It's just physical. After Christmas, we go back to our regularly scheduled lives where we don't talk to each other and you can go back to hating me."

"I still do hate you," she says with a grin. "You're a dick, remember?"

I sit back and pull her up with me, settling her on top of me. She straddles me and steadies herself against my shoulders.

"You want to see a dick, Lana. Just ask," I say, thrusting my hips against her. She rubs herself over the length of me and I'm desperate to feel her take my cock.

"You think you're such a stud, don't you?" she asks, eyes hooded and looking down at me.

"I'm not the one riding my cock like it's the best thing you've ever had," I say into her neck.

"Just promise me you won't say anything to Vance," she says, stopping her hips.

"About?"

"This," she hisses.

"Oh, you don't want me to tell your brother that I fucked his sister while he slept off his drunken night?"

She slaps my chest. "You haven't fucked me," she says.

"No," I shake my head and then reach for her throat, pulling her lips down to mine. "But I'm about to."

Now in one swift motion I rip off the shirt that she's wearing and she looks down and watches as the buttons go flying into the air all around us. Her eyes widen as she looks at me, and I take in the sight of the white lace bra. She looks like a snow angel.

"What's wrong, baby?" I say looking at her she stares back at me dumbfounded.

"Did you just rip my shirt?" she asks, incredulously.

"How else was I going to bind your hands and cover your eyes?" I tug the material down her arms, and before she has a chance to protest I flip her and she's now in my spot.

"Hands on the back of the couch," I tell her.

"What are you—"

"You told me what you wanted, Lana. It's midnight, which means it's officially Christmas eve and since you've been a bad girl... I think you know exactly what kind of present you're getting."

She stares up at me, those beautiful full lips of hers pouting.

"Don't do that," I warn her, running a thumb down her lips. "The more you pout, the more it makes me want to drive my cock into your sexy mouth. Now turn around. Be a good girl for once and do as your told."

I'm pleased when she reluctantly flips herself around and puts her hands on the back of the couch.

"Lean forward," I instruct her. "Ass up."

Her bright red silk shorts, stretch out over ass cheeks and—*my god*—I want to just feast on her.

But not yet.

I rip the silk pajama top into strips. One, thicker than the other two. I grab the thicker one and lean forward, using it to cover her eyes. I tie it around the back of her head and secure it in place.

Then I grab one of the smaller strips and tie her ankles together. I tug on it to make sure it won't come loose, before rounding the couch and tying her wrists together again.

Hello, my beautiful angel. The sight of her ready and waiting for me, springs my already hard erection to life.

If I'll only get to experience Lana in this cabin, while her brother sleeps. Then I'll need to take advantage of the short amount of time we have together.

And by the time we have to leave, I'll make sure she thinks twice about going back to the way things were before we got here.

I reach for her lips and she breathes out.

"You look so good, waiting for me," I tell her, bending down to kiss her full lips. She kisses me back, hungry and excited.

I straighten and go back around to where her tight little ass is propped up. I put both my hands on her waist and pull her shorts down slowly. Waiting for me underneath them is a matching thong to go with the lace bra. White against her copper skin. Such a fucking sight.

Since her ankles are already tied, I can't slip the shorts off the entire way so I just leave them pooled at her knees. Next, I reach for the lace fabric giving it a nice tug so that she feels it against her clit.

She whimpers. And it makes me so happy to see this tough woman, weak for me. I shouldn't like it so much. But I'll bet if the tables were turned and she had me tied up because that's what she likes, I'd be just as turned on.

She wants this. She gets this.

I get on my knees behind her and bring my mouth to the roundness of her cheeks. "You are so goddamn beautiful, angel."

"What happend to little grinch?" she chuckles.

"Oh you're still my little grinch, but right now, dressed in these," I tug on the fabric some more and she squirms slightly. "You're my snow angel."

I kiss her on each of her cheeks. "And I can't wait to see how pink these will turn for me, once I'm done with them."

"Oh," she breathes out.

"Are you ready, angel?"

She nods enthusiastically and I ready my hand for the first swat.

Chapter 9
Lana

There aren't many things that I'm afraid of. I learned early on in life that you need to be tough. Expect the unexpected, and always, *always* be the one with the plan.

It was a necessary and exhausting existence. Which is why I think I harbor these secret fantasies.

For once, I want to be the one getting chased. I want to be the one being told what to do. Someone, for all that is holy, take the reigns because–gosh, it's so exhausting.

So yeah... I want to relinquish control. I want someone else to have a plan. And Trevor Sincaid, as irritating as I find him to be, just flipped the script on me.

"You're sure?" he asks one more time.

"Yes," I whisper, my eyes covered by the silk of my top, hands and ankles bound and ass out for him. "Do it."

He swats my backside and the pain, stinging and fierce shoots across the nerves on my body. My core pulses and my breathing grows ragged.

"I'm going to do it, again. Are you okay, Angel?"

Angel. Not little grinch. Not Vance's sister. *Angel.*

"Yes," I whimper.

I don't mean for my voice to sound like that. But I didn't know how badly I needed this, until this very moment. To just be wanted, taken, completely worshipped.

His hand swats my other cheek and I lurch forward on the couch. That one was louder, and I wonder if we're being too loud.

The last thing I want is for my brother to come down the hall to find us like this.

I would never be able to live down that humiliation.

Trevor's hand rubs the spot where he just hit. "Your skin is so perfect," he whispers to me in awe.

It's just loud enough that the roaring fire behind us, nearly drowns him out. His other hand comes up and rubs both my cheeks. I love the feeling of his calloused hands on my skin. Hot and rough.

"Do it again," I say into the darkness.

He does, swats me two more times, rubbing both cheeks again and this when he finishes he reaches up and pinches my nipples, the pain of my ass being spanked combined with the sensation of his fingers on my nipples makes me gasp.

"Does that hurt?" he asks, concern lacing his voice.

"No," I breathe. "It feels so good."

He moves one hand from my breast and slides it in between my thighs finding my throbbing clit and spreading my arousal over myself. "You're so wet, Angel. I love feeling you like this."

My body relaxes at his touch and I moan my pleasure, ever so lightly.

"We can't be too loud," I say, mostly to myself.

"No," he chuckles. "We can't." He picks up the pace and I can feel my orgasm building, about to slam into me.

It's like riding a wave and knowing you can't stop until it's crashed against the shore.

"You are so fucking beautiful," he says, his lips are on my ass again and I can feel him sucking my skin into his mouth as his fingers work magic.

The sensation sends me over the edge and I buck against his hand, grinding down hard as I drench him in all my arousal, my face planted into the couch cushions as I catch my breath.

My god, that was amazing. And I don't want it to end. I need more.

"I'm not done with you, Lana. If you come all over my hand so beautifully, I can't wait to see how you take my cock, Angel."

"Mmmm," I hum against bound hands.

"Is that what you want? To come all over my cock?" The sound of his voice, thick with need sends shivers up my spine.

"Yes," I say.

"Yes, what, Angel?"

"Yes... I want to come all over your cock," I say.

Trevor chuckles. Deep and throaty. "That's what I thought. Because I'm going to need to hear the sounds you make when I'm driving into you, Angel. But before I do that.."

He flips me over and I'm now on my back. He situates himself between my legs and pulls my core closer to him. I can feel that rock hard erection in his pants and I grind over it.

"Uh-uh," he says. "Not until I say so."

He then yanks my thong down my leg and dips his head between my thighs. The binds on my ankles only let me move so much. But I feel his hair tickling the sensitive skin there as his tongue laps me up from clit to ass. He doesn't waste a single drop.

And when he's done licking me up, he focuses on that sensitive nub again, but this time, he uses his tongue.

"You like that, don't you?" he says onto my skin, nipping and licking as I buck into his face.

"Yes," I say softly. He stays face-planted against that spot and then brings a finger up to my entrance.

"Good, because I'm going to fuck you with my fingers until you're begging for my cock, Angel. So don't you dare come. You hear me?"

Excuse me, don't come?!

He's working magic with his tongue already and plans to finger fuck me into oblivion, but I'm not allowed to come.

"How is that fair?" I breathe out, his tongue picking up speed.

"Because the more you come, the more you'll get tired. And if I only get you for a little bit, Lana... I'm going to have you to the fullest."

That will do.

"Okay," I say. "But I want to see you. I want to see what your face looks like buried between my legs."

"Now that is fair," he says. He reaches for my impromptu eye mask, and I can finally see him. Hair mussed, eyes hungry. And he looks up at me with those light, golden eyes and licks me lazily like I'm a dessert he's trying his best to savor.

I close my eyes, because the sight of him is too much.

"No, Angel. Open your eyes and watch me fuck you."

My eyes fly open and I watch as he picks up speed, his fingers moving in and out of my dripping cunt as his tongue continues to suck and tease and flick against my clit.

"I don't think I can take it," I say.

"Yes," he says, gruffly. "You can take it, Lana. You can take this and more because by the time I'm done with you... you're going to wish you had more."

What he doesn't know is that I already do. This is the best sex I've ever had and he hasn't even fully fucked me yet. How am I supposed to just go about my day tomorrow knowing that this is what I've been missing out on.

I feel the wave building again.

No. I can't come.

"Stop!" I breathe out.

And without questioning me, he does.

His fingers pull out of me, leaving me feeling empty and his tongue stops it's epic assault on my clit as he looks up at me.

Pleased, the corners of his mouth lift up into a grin.

"That was very good, Angel. Save it for me."

I let out a shattered breath because, this man—fuck—he's making me feel so much more alive than I've felt... well, ever.

I swallow hard as he releases the binds from my ankles. He leaves the ones on my wrists, but takes me into his arms and carries me over to kitchen. He sets me on top of the kitchen island and reaches behind snapping my bra off.

"I want to see all of you when I take you," he says, tossing my bra over his shoulder.

"Do you have a—"

He reaches into his back pocket and produces a shiny, silver packet.

"Looking for this?"

"For someone who hasn't had sex in so long, you sure are prepared."

"Well, I didn't want to tell you this because I'm sure

you'd think I'm a perv. But I bought a box at the mini-mart in town."

I cock my head at him. "So you were planning on seducing me."

"Lana, I took one look at you and I knew I was a goner."

"Well you have a weird way of showing it," I say.

He reaches for the waistband of his joggers and slips them down his thick thighs. And there it is. That bulging erection that has made my head swim in dirty thoughts all day.

"Is this a weird way of showing it?" He steps out of his sweats and kicks them aside before coming in between my legs.

"Allow me, stud," I say, taking the condom from his hand and ripping it open with my mouth.

I take hold of his erection and pull it toward me. He grunts at the motion and watches me through hooded eyes.

My wrists still bound, I take his cock in one hand while I roll the condom onto the head of it with the other and then use both to roll it over him entirely.

He shakes his head. "I'm thoroughly impressed. Now lay back, arms over your head."

I lean back just as he lines up at my entrance. And I feel my body light up with excitement.

He pushes into me, swirling the head of his cock against my wetness and pushes in some more. It takes a few tries, but once he's fully seated in me he lets out a bated breath.

"You feel... heavenly," he whispers.

"Then fuck me," I say.

Chapter 10
Trevor

Feeling her tense around my cock, I can't help but pound into her. She takes me so well it makes me crazy.

I watch as her tits bounce with each thrust and I already know that now that I've felt what it feels like to have Lana's cunt swallowing me whole—I don't know how I'm ever going to be able to not think about her.

I move slow at first, but then she tells me to go harder and I grab her thighs, my thumbs digging into her as I do and I meet her thrust for thrust.

She's still bound by the wrists, her arms above her head laying back on the kitchen island.

And the view is so perfect.

"I'm going to touch you," I grit out, doing my best to maintain my composure.

"And you'll be good and not scream when I pound you into oblivion while rubbing your sweet beautiful clit, right Angel?"

I thrust into her.

"Right," she breathes out. "Yes. Please."

"Such good manners." I reach for her clit and spread the moisture there as I watch my cock glide in and out, in and out. She bucks up into me and bites down hard on her lip. And I know I won't last long at all.

Her pussy has me in a chokehold and just before I'm about to stop she pulses around my cock and brings her hands to her mouth screaming out.

I reach forward, taking a hold of her throat and wrapping one hand around it as I use the other on her clit and keep thrusting into her.

She writhes but now with my hand on her throat she gasps instead of screams.

"That's my good." Thrust. "Fucking." Thrust. "Girl." I spill into her and don't take my hand off her throat as I do, lifting her up so that our faces meet and her lips are on mine, swallowing my own groans as I come into her.

My head spins and it's not until I feel her gulp against my hand that I realize I'm still holding her throat.

I quickly move it and she takes in a deep breath.

"Holy shit, are you okay?"

I slide out of her and take her face into both my hands.

"Yes," she breathes. "That was... just wow."

I swallow, trying to catch my own breath.

"I didn't hurt you, did I?"

She looks down between her thighs, and I can see I left marks there. And I know for sure I left marks on her ass.

"Shit," I say, bringing a hand up to my face.

"I'm so sorry, Lana."

"No." She shakes her head. "No, that was amazing, Trevor. I've never..."

"You've never what?"

"I've never let myself be taken like that."

"Well, to be fair... I've never done that."

She looks at me, in disbelief. "Really? I find that hard to believe."

I roll the condom and tie it off before tossing it into the trash and I grab my pants and slip them back on.

"Well, I'm glad you think so. I just wanted to make you feel good."

She smiles. "Well, mission accomplished. That was incredible."

She holds her wrists out for me. "Do you mind?"

I stand between her legs and take her bound wrists into my hands, working gently to get her untied.

"You'd tell me if I was too rough, right?' I say, looking into her eyes. "Your brother did make sure to emphasize that I shouldn't hurt you."

She chuckles. "Trevor, I'm pretty sure he didn't mean it in this context."

I shrug. "He didn't specify, so..."

"He can't know anything happened between us," she reiterates.

"Yeah, you've made that pretty clear."

"Good."

I get the fabric loosened and set it down next to her. She massages her wrists as I go grab her clothes and hand them to her.

She slides off the kitchen island and looks at me.

"What?"

"You seem upset," she says, studying me.

I shake my head. "Nope. If you're good, then I'm good."

She reaches for my hand and looks at me. "We just did something very... intimate," she says. "Please don't just shut down on me."

I swallow past that uncomfortable feeling in my throat.

"I'm going to take a shower. And then I'll meet you in the room, okay?"

She nods. "Okay."

I pick up the pieces of the fabric I ripped up and take them with me.

No good leaving any evidence for her brother to find in the morning.

My body is finally giving in to the lack of sleep. I feel the fatigue overtake me as I undress and step into the steam shower.

Was I upset in the kitchen? I guess I was. It doesn't feel good for anyone to reject you especially after you've given them a part of yourself.

Lana's been hurt. She's no doubt been taken for granted. I can understand if she's guarding herself from any future pain.

And it's not like we really got off to a good start. I can't expect her to just fully embrace me, she doesn't even know me. And I don't know her.

But I want to.

Maybe that's the difference. Lana has no interest in getting to know me. And I have every intention of seeing where things can go.

I let the water run over my face and my tired body. Maybe in the morning, I'll be able think clearer. Once the fog of lust as she called it, has lifted.

The shower door swings open and I turn to find her standing there, fully naked in front of me.

"Didn't you already shower?" I ask.

"I mean, we kind of made a mess out there," she says, smiling up at me. "Besides, we need to talk."

She reaches behind me and squirts some soap into hand lathering it up.

"Turn around," she says.

I look at her. "You gonna spank me, now?" I say, quirking a brow.

"No, I'm going to wash you. Turn around."

I gulp. Nobody's ever washed me. But I do, giving her my back and resting my hands on the shower glass.

Her hands touch my skin and once again my body comes alive for her. I don't know why I have this reaction to her. She told me we only get tonight. And I know this can't be more. So maybe I just want everything she'll give me.

"I was going to marry one of Vance's childhood friends," she says softly.

I still. Because for the first time since meeting her, she's actually opening up.

"We had been on and off for years. I had the biggest crush on him growing up. He was just the kind of guy that gave off this aura that he was untouchable. Unattainable. All the girls wanted to get with him. It was kind of annoying."

She lathers the soap against my skin. And I love how her hands feel on me.

"But I was the lucky one that got to spend the most time with him since he and V were so close, you know? Eventually we grew up. I caught his eye. And we dated. It was supposed to be my happily ever after."

"So what happened?" I say, turning to look at her. She keeps washing me. Her hands now roaming my chest and abs.

"I found out on my wedding day, that he never stopped being the guy that all the girls wanted. He overslept during his bachelor party and didn't show up to our wedding."

"He overslept?" I ask.

"Oh yeah, with two of my bridesmaids, no less."

My shoulders slump and I look at the broken woman in front of me. "Lana... you didn't deserve that."

She shakes her head. "No. I didn't." Her eyes meet mine, sad and overcome with tears.

"I'm sorry that happened."

She shrugs. "It wasn't your fault. I'd just heard all these rumors about you and the second I realized who you were I just thought I was being forced into the same story all over again. This guy that I find very attractive but could never be."

She's still moving her hands over my body, but I take her wrists and force her to look at me.

"I would never do that, Lana. Whatever rumors you've heard, that's all they are—*rumors*. That's not who I am."

"I know," she says, her voice breaking. "I think I know that now. And honestly, it's scary to admit, because... I feel like all these walls I've built up around my heart. Around love. You're breaking them... just by being you."

"I hope so," I say, pulling her to me and wrapping her into an embrace.

She's much smaller than me, she fits perfectly into my body. I rest my head on her hair and breathe her in.

"I don't do things like this," she says.

"Neither do I," I admit.

"But... I feel like I'd be missing out on something big if I didn't at least see this through." She looks up at me.

"What are you saying?" I ask her, pulling away just a bit.

"Trevor, when we get back..." her lashes flutter as the water hits her. "Do you want to go out with me?"

I look down at her. *Did I just hear her correctly?* "Wait, are you seriously asking me out?"

She bites her lip and nods. "Yes."

"You really are a feminist aren't you?"

She slaps my chest and laughs. "Just answer the question."

I take her by the chin and kiss her. "Yes, Lana. I'd love nothing more than to go out with you."

She smiles against my lips. "Good. Because that can't be the last time we ever have sex. That was way too good!"

I pinch her ass and pull her close to me, our tongues dancing against each other as the water pours down our bodies.

"Then let's fix that, right away." I lift her up, her legs wrapping around my waist as I push her up against the glass.

She moans against my lips. "Let's."

Epilogue
New Years Eve | Lana

"Let me get this straight. You want me to go in there, dressed in that and get mocked by a bunch of thirteen year old girls," Trevor says, pointing at the Ice Queens team mascot costume.

Rina Lopez looks at me and I just shrug.

"I'm guessing you didn't tell him," she says.

Once we decided to go on a date, it didn't take long for the Heatwave fans to spot us around town. The little debacle with the calendar quickly got replaced with rumors of "The Rookie" hooking up with his teammate's sister.

A rumor that was true. Very, *very* true.

But Rina had reached out to me before Christmas and told me that one of her players needed some community service hours. So without even knowing him, I had volunteered him to be the mascot for some of our home games in the new year.

"It's not as bad as he's making it out to be," I say.

Trevor cocks his head at me.

"He'll be a natural lady snow leopard," I assure them both.

Izzy, Trevor's ex and the Heatwave team photographer, comes up to us with her camera.

"I gotta admit. I've been waiting for the day when Trevor Sincaid would get his mascot debut."

She winks at me. Then snaps photos of him as he suits up, the long fluffy tail swinging out and nearly hitting us.

"Who usually wears this thing?" Trevor says, slipping the head of it on, topped with a crown and all.

"That would be me," my brother says, coming up behind me. "Sorry I'm late. I wanted to make sure the guys knew where to go."

"What guys?" Trevor says from inside the suit.

The doors burst open and the Heatwave starting lineup and a few of the others on the roster come in wearing Ice Queen jerseys, drinks and popcorn in hand.

"You invited the whole team?" Trevor says, arms trying to cross in the suit.

"I didn't invite them," I say.

"I did," Mick admits.

"Don't worry," Our team captain approaches. "We came to watch the Ice Queens take down the Storm. I heard it's the hockey rivalry of the year."

"Thanks for coming," I tell them.

"No problem, coach," Keelan says, saluting me. The guys all take the seats near the opposing team's bench and start chirping at the other team.

The Storm team coach looks at me arms raised in question.

"Sorry," I mouth to her.

"Alright, Rookie," Rina tells him. "You're up."

The music starts and the small crowd gathered comes to life as Trevor walks up to me and squeezes me into a hug.

"I'll be back," he says through the mascot head.

The girls I coach line up to get onto the ice behind us.

"Ew, is that your boyfriend?" One of them asks.

Trevor turns to the little forward.

"Yes! This beautiful, intelligent, incredible woman is *my* girlfriend," Trevor says, hugging me close to his side. "And I'm the luckiest snow leopard in all the land."

He takes a theatrical bow and the girls all give each other looks.

"I swear he's much cooler outside of this costume," I assure them.

They laugh, but as soon as the announcer comes on, Trevor does a few jumping jacks and runs out onto the ice.

The Heatwave players go nuts at the sight of their team-mate and popcorn goes flying everywhere.

Our games are never this exciting, but as my now boyfriend starts dancing on the ice—I notice the seats filling up in the arena.

"Is it just me?" I turn to Rina, "Or is this place getting pretty packed."

"You can thank the guys for that. They've been posting about this game and getting the fans to come out to support girl's hockey."

My heart swells. This is what my girls deserve. This is what the sport needs. Fans that are thrilled to support.

I watch my lady leopard go full heart on the ice pumping up the crowd. It was supposed to be a punishment for him. But he's enjoying it way too much. And honestly, I'm glad he's not treating it like a punishment—he's treating it like a privilege.

His entire team is.

And it gives me so much hope for the future.

He finishes his dance and the girls take their place on the ice and the fans go even wilder for them.

"How'd I do?" he asks, bouncing back to me.

"You rocked that suit. In fact, maybe you should keep it on."

He growls and pinches my butt, making me yelp.

"Anything to keep that smile on your face, my little grinch."

I drop the smile.

"My little snow Angel," he corrects himself.

"That's better," I mutter with a smirk.

"Now, get out there and coach your little heart out. Because later, it's my turn," he says.

"You know, it's really hard to take you seriously when you look like that."

"If I tie you up will you take me more seriously?"

I think about it for all of two seconds. "Yes, yes I will."

"Good, because when the clock strikes twelve... you're all mine," he growls.

The love doesn't end here...

This was just a little taste of the Heatwave players. If you haven't read the series—start with Pucked Together. It's a brother's best friend romance with all the laughs and love from our Heatwave boys.

Read Pucked Together or any of the other Heatwave books on Amazon here!

Follow Anne Martin on Amazon to stay up to date on all new releases.

Also by Anne Martin

Heatwave Hockey Series

Pucked Together

Damaged Defender

Offensive Plays

Scoring Chances

Penalty Shots

Holiday Power Play

Cedar Grove Series

My Best Friend's Billionaire Brother

Neighbor's Secret Baby

Secret Billionaire Protector

Silver Fox Boss

Standalones

Baby for Brother's Best Friend